JAZZ

JAZZ

Nature's Improvisation

Elizabeth Copeland

QUATTRO BOOKS

The publication of *Jazz* has been generously supported by
the Canada Council for the Arts and the Ontario Arts Council.

 Canada Council   Conseil des arts
for the Arts   du Canada

 ONTARIO ARTS COUNCIL
CONSEIL DES ARTS DE L'ONTARIO
an Ontario government agency
un organisme du gouvernement de l'Ontario

Author photo: B. Glenn-Copeland
Cover design: Sarah Beaudin
Typography: Diane Mascherin
Editor: Luciano Iacobelli

Library and Archives Canada Cataloguing in Publication

Copeland, Elizabeth, author
    Jazz : nature's improvisation / Elizabeth Copeland.

ISBN 978-1-927443-65-1 (pbk.)

    1. Transgender people--Fiction. I. Title.

PS8605.O6794J39 2014   C813'.6   C2014-905787-3

Published by Quattro Books Inc.
Toronto
info@quattrobooks.ca
www.quattrobooks.ca

Printed in Canada

DEDICATION

Mr. Cartmail was one of those rare teachers who not only made me want to think, but earned my trust and love as well. When halfway into the academic year, he was dismissed, the rumours started flying, and within a few weeks the word was out. Mr. Cartmail had been fired because he was gay. I never saw Mr. Cartmail again, and don't know anything about how the rest of his life played out. But I do know that losing him in this way woke me up to the unspeakable costs we pay – as individuals and as a society – to justify and perpetuate our prejudices.

TRANS: *from the Latin meaning to cross, go beyond*

GENDER: *(French from the Latin* genus*: a kind), the behavioural, cultural or psychological traits associated with one sex*

TRANSGENDER: *of, relating to, or being a person who identifies with or expresses a gender identity that differs from the one which corresponds to the person's sex at birth*

There is a shadow of a girl floating around me. Gossamer. Guileless. I pretend I do not see her. She embarrasses me. Though I have tried, I cannot unlearn or forget what her life in me has given. And taken. Mostly taken.

There is a shadow of a boy walking within me. Ferocious. Fine. Though his heart breaks and mends, breaks and mends, and breaks again, he will not be shackled. His spirit is lightning fire.

At birth, I was labeled a girl. I was named Jaswinder.

My chosen name is Jazz. Like the music, I am nature's improvisation.

TRANSFORM: *(French from Latin), to change the form of*

I told my mother I was a boy when I was four years old. She was standing at the counter, grinding the spices for the evening meal. Curry. Cumin. Garamasala. She stopped. Sighed. Turned and smiled at me, her mouth tense.

"Don't be foolish, Jaswinder. Now, run along and wash your hands before dinner."

I told her again when I was twelve. We were in her sewing room. Bolts of brilliantly hued fabric were stacked against one wall. Straight pins and needles stood gaily on a green satin pincushion. Thimbles, scissors, pinking sheers. All neatly in their place. A chest full of tiny drawers, each containing threads of different colour, stood beside the picture window that overlooked our backyard. I could see the branches of the willow tree, waving at me as they danced in the wind.

"Close the door, Jaswinder." She began slowly. Her voice soft. Choosing her words carefully. Wanting to say just the right thing. To convince me of the sacred wonder of it all. Of womanhood.

I didn't want to interrupt her at first, to take this moment away from her. After all, I was her only daughter. Clearly she had put a lot of effort into this speech, considered deeply how much or how little to tell me about the changes my body was going through. But in the midst of her detailed explanation, I stopped her.

"Mother, I would rather die than to grow up to be a woman."

Her back stiffened.

"What foolishness is this? As if you have any choice in the matter."

I told her again today. At my seventeenth birthday party.

In front of my whole family – the aunties and uncles, the cousins, my friend, Jennie from high school, and my big brother, Sugith.

After they brought out the presents and sang Happy Birthday.

Just as my mother was about to cut the homemade carrot cake with cream cheese icing. My favourite.

The smile falls from her face. She drops the knife on the floor. Nobody moves. My brother looks away. Disgusted.

"I always knew you were a freak."

"Enough, Sugith." My father struggles to keep his voice under control. "Jaswinder. Look how you have upset your mother. This is not something we joke about."

"It's not a joke."

Freeze frame. No one knows where to look. At my brother's twisted face? At my mother, her eyes wide in an attempt to stop the tears that threaten? Or at my father, standing still and hard as granite?

On some unspoken cue, my aunties begin to fuss around my mother. A gaggle of hens, scratching and clucking. Picking up the knife from the floor. Cleaning the icing off the carpet. Straightening up the already tidy table.

"Come with me." Auntie Nazneen hisses in my ear. "NOW!" She pulls me from the room. Through the French doors and onto the deck. "Go to your mother. Apologize at once!"

"No."

"What did you say?"

"No."

We wait until everyone leaves. Which doesn't take long. Amazing how fast you can clear a room with a simple announcement.

The door is shut and bolted. The window shades drawn. Auntie Nazneen and my mother scuttle from the room. I am left alone with my father. He is standing by the window with his hands clasped behind his back. Looking out. Seeing nothing. A storm is coming. But there is no escaping it. It is time. Deep breath in. *Just relax. I can do this.*

"Jaswinder, what is the meaning of this behaviour?"

"Father, I…"

My mother peeks out from the kitchen. Quietly shakes her head. Mouths the word *no*.

I stop. The air around me crackles. A warning light goes on in my brain. A flashing sign. *No more pretending. No more pretending.*

I swallow hard. *Remember the words!* Words I have learned from books. From thousands of hours of research on the Internet. Words that have helped me sew myself together. Like Peter Pan and his shadow, except I do not have a Wendy to help me.

No going back after this. My hand on the lever, I pause. Check my anger. Remember. *A reasonable approach will elicit a reasonable response.* I open my throat to say aloud the words I have been practicing for years. Open the gates of the dam. The words flood out.

"Father. Mother. Today is a reason to both mourn and celebrate. To mourn the loss of a daughter. And to celebrate that you have another son."

It sounded so good in rehearsal. In my bedroom. In front of the mirror. Now it sounds forced.

The blood drains from my mother's face. Her jaw hangs open. She looks older by years than she did just an hour ago.

My father turns his head. Regards me from the corner of his eye. No longer is there kindness, infinite patience, the dry humour that could send me into paroxysms of laughter.

"So let me understand this. You are gay. A lesbian."

"No father, I am…" *The words. The words. Where are the words?* "I am…transgendered. I am a man."

He looks at me. Sees a stranger. Laughs bitterly.

"You are no more a man than I am a fish."

A flash of lightning. Of understanding. *It's not working.* The ground is shifting under my feet. I repeat the mantra in my head. *A reasonable approach will elicit a reasonable response.*

Then, riding into the rescue comes take-charge Nazneen. Commanding attention. Demanding compliance.

"Chemim. Amarjit. Jaswinder. Come into the kitchen. We will have tea. We will talk as a family. We will work this out."

My father does not move.

"Amarjit, please." My mother's voice. Broken. "She is your daughter."

"I no longer have a daughter." A low rumble of thunder.

"Brother, not so fast." Said sweetly. Auntie Nazneen. The mediator. Calming the waters. "I agree it is shocking. But it is just a phase that she will grow out of. I am sure of that."

Thunder cracks. The lowering sky opens. "Enough, Nazneen!"

Silence hangs heavy in the air. Then a sound. Choking. Terrifying in its vulnerability. My father is weeping.

"My daughter is lost."

Synapses firing at lightning speed, I scroll down, scanning in my head through the articles, through the lists of topics, the headings, searching for the answer to the question, *What to do if your parents disown you.*

I walk towards my father. To offer comfort. My feet leaden. Dragging an anvil out to sea.

"No father. Not lost."

"Not lost," my mother echoes.

He turns on her. "Tell your daughter to end this nonsense. Or tell her to leave this house forever."

Winds like a monsoon blow a torrent of rain. I am betrayed. Betrayed! Betrayed by the words that promised my salvation.

The room is airless. No one moves from their frozen tableau.

We all wait. For the storm to pass over. For someone to save the ship from dashing on the rocks.

My mother makes her move. Chooses her side.

"You must go, Jaswinder."

Moving to the front door, she flips the deadbolt. Opens the door. *A reasonable approach will elicit a reasonable response. It is not too late.* I take her hand. Pet it.

"Mother. Listen to me. I want you to understand…" I inhale her familiar scent. Lavender.

She shakes my hand away. Hisses bitterness. "Understand what? That you have taken leave of your senses? That you think you are a man? That is craziness. Do you not understand that we must accept the way we are made?" She strikes to wound. "Do you not understand that you are killing your father?"

Auntie Nazneen steps in, in her new role as judge, jury and executioner. "You must go from this house. Do not argue. We are decided."

Blow winds. Blow. Drop the sails. Turn the bow into the wind.

"I am a man. This is how I was born. I cannot change that."

"This is NOT how you were born." My father, in a rare fit of temper, stands. Picks up an antique vase that has been in the family for hundreds of years. Aims. Hurls it to the floor at my feet, where it shatters into tiny pieces.

Wiping the tears from her cheeks, my mother steps towards me. Pushes a lock of hair back from my forehead. Holds my face in her hands. One word. "Go."

This is surreal, like a scene from the Commedia dell'arte.

My aunt. *La Signora*. Obscenely made up. Eyes averted. Ridiculously proud.

My father. *Il Dottore*. Half his face masked. His body padded with anger.

My mother. A female *Pierrot*. Trusting. White faced. Heartbroken.

I move in slow motion, articulating every move to give them time to change their minds.

I take a windbreaker to protect me from the rain. *Pierrot* turns away.

I grab one of the envelopes on the table – a gift of money from my Auntie Nazneen. *La Signora* sneers.

I exit. Turn. Waiting. *Il Dottore* strides forward, his robes billowing behind him. One final cutting look.

Slam.

My first stop is Zellers to buy scissors. Then to a change room. The scissors are cheap and I am sawing rather than cutting off the long, black hair that my mother loved. I should keep it. Put it in an envelope. Send it to her as a parting shot. Instead I leave it on the floor for the next customer. A gift. To commemorate the last time I will ever enter a ladies change room.

A plan. I need a plan. I call my friend, Jennie. We've been friends since middle school. She'll help me.

She picks up her phone right away. Sounding distant. Irritated.

"Jazz. What the heck was that?"

"What do you mean? You know about me. Did you think I could live a lie all my life?"

"No, not all your life. But at least until you got through university and had a job."

All through high school, Jennie and I kind of had a thing for each other, though she would never let me touch her. Now I wonder if maybe the attraction was one-sided. Mine alone. Maybe I was just a token weirdo friend.

"Where are you anyway?'

"They threw me out." Silence. "Can you help me?"

These are the make it or break it moments in a friendship. She'll either back me up or cut me loose.

I hear her sharpening her knife. "What do you expect from me?"

"Can I stay at your house? Sleep in your basement for a few days, until I figure out what to do?"

I feel it. One of her hands grabbing the rope. The other, positioning it for a swift cut.

"My parents would freak out. You should go home. Tell them you're sorry, that you're stressed. I don't know. I…"

I decide to release her from her suffering. Tell her to put down the knife. "Don't worry. I'll be okay. Look, there's the bus. I have to go." I hang up before she can say good-bye. Now what?

I'll go to Church Street and talk to the guy who works at the Second Cup. *What was his name? Jarred? Jacob?* A friendly guy. He'll help. I know he'll help.

~

Every Saturday afternoon for the last year, I have been hanging out on Church Street. *The Land of the Fay, and the Home of the Queers.* That is what my brother calls it.

Church and Wellesley. The heart of Toronto's LGBT community. Sidewalks crowded with people all talking loudly and enthusiastically at once – a symphony of world language, punctuated by the occasional staccato rant of some tortured soul lost in the tunnels of their own loneliness. Artists. Academics. Poor people. Rich people. Old. Young.

Gay. Straight. And everything in between. A world apart.
Where I can relax. Be myself.

I see my reflection in a window outside of Zellers. With my
hair short, I may just have a chance in hell of passing as a
guy.

I jump on the bus. Find a seat in the back where I can
sit alone. Where I can think. Where I can enjoy this final ride
from my past into my future.

I swallow the knot of fear that sits like a golf ball in
my throat. Time to take stock of what I have. I dig down into
my back pocket. Feel the envelope that was Auntie's gift. Pull
it out. Rip it open and count. One hundred dollars.

What else do I have? Three tokens. A ten-dollar bill.
Two loonies. Three quarters and a dime. A penknife. My
library card. My health card. My cell phone. Half-charged.
And no charger.

I check the pockets of the black windbreaker. Five
dollars. A few pennies. A coupon for Burger King. A half
pack of Trident gum. Mint. And a paperback.

On the subway platform, I flip open the book and
begin to read. Perfect. A book about Thomas Cromwell.
Overarching ambition. Nefarious plotting. Betrayal. All
leading to a rise to power, and then. Off with his head! A bad
omen. I leave it on a seat in the subway car when I get off at
Yonge station.

TRANSVALUE: *to reevaluate according to new principles, repudiating the current prevailing standards*

CHEMIM

When my daughter Jaswinder told me she was a boy, I immediately called up my sister-in-law Nazneen to ask her advice. She was vacationing in Tuscany with her white C.E.O. husband, and I didn't like to bother her. But there was no one else I could talk to.

I pictured her sitting on a terrace up in the hills, sipping a cool drink and dressed in something light and colourful.

"Chemim, you must not make too much of this. I have read about these things. It is just a phase. She will grow out of it."

"Are you sure?"

"Oh yes. But do not under any circumstances tell my brother."

So I did as Nazneen told me. I did not insist on proper behaviour for a girl, and I let her dress and act as a tomboy.

It was hard not to love her as she was, and she was so happy. So I let it go on.

For her seventh birthday, her father and I bought her a Jessica doll. They were all the rage, and most of the girls in her class had one. Three months later, I found the doll under her bed, her hair cut off, its blue and white gingham dress ripped to shreds, and its eyes poked out.

I called Nazneen to tell her what happened.

"The phase is not passing as you said it would. What am I to do?"

"She is only seven years old. Do not worry."

Once again, I did as she said. I brushed it all from my mind. I stopped trying to interest her in frilly clothes and jewelry, and just let her be.

16

Jaswinder was a good student, always bringing home high marks. She loved to read, and when she was not out running wild with her *buddies*, as she called them, she usually had her nose in a book.

Her body began to change at age eleven, and so did she, and not for the good. She was most often in a bad temper and there was lots of door slamming in the house. She started wearing big, baggy clothes to cover herself and on the day of her first period, she flew into a rage.

In the months that followed, she became like a hermit, going straight to her room after school and staying there for hours. I shouted up the stairs. "Why don't you call one of your buddies and see if they want to come over to watch a movie?"

She shouted down, "We're not friends anymore."

Nazneen told me I had to put my foot down.

"Tell her that she must develop some interests and that she cannot spend all her time in her room!"

To my surprise, Jaswinder listened. Every Saturday, rain or shine, she walked the four blocks to our local library and spent the afternoon. When she became secretive about what she was reading, I chalked it up to the normal teenage need for privacy.

One Saturday she did not come home for dinner at the usual time. I was worried. I didn't want to upset Amarjit, so I told her him she was with a friend. The hours went by. I became angry. Then frightened. A young woman was not safe on the streets. It was almost dark by the time she got home.

"The library closed hours ago. Where were you?"

She shrugged her shoulders in the way I had come to hate.

"Nowhere special. With Jennie."

I did not believe it. The next morning I called Jennie's mother. Asked for a recipe. Inquired after her daughter.

"Jennie is away this weekend. Visiting her cousins in Hamilton." Aha!

17

A mother must know what is going on with her child, so the next Saturday afternoon I went to the library. My daughter was not there. I asked Mrs. Czerny, the librarian, a good woman I had known for many years, if she knew anything.

"I don't want to get her into trouble."

"There will be no trouble." But of course there would be.

"She comes in every Saturday, returns her books, checks out new books, and then changes her clothing and leaves."

I did not ask the librarian to tell me what clothing she changed into. I did not want to know.

I did not go home. I waited at the bus stop near the library for one hour. Then two. Then three. Shortly before five o'clock, I saw my daughter step down from the bus. I recognized the clothes she was wearing – Sugith's clothes, baggy jeans tied up with a piece of leather, a black t-shirt with a GAP logo, and a hoodie pulled up over her long hair. I could not believe my eyes. The back of my neck burned in shame.

I pulled the car onto the curb beside her. I was so upset I almost hit another pedestrian.

"I know what you are doing. Get in." I wanted to strike her.

We rode in silence all the way home. Though I did not intend to tell my husband what I knew, I did threaten to tell him what she was doing, and how she had brought shame on our family. She loved her father and I knew that would keep her in her place.

She stayed home every Saturday for the next four years. Her grades went down, she stopped eating, and she no longer talked to me with love.

AMARJIT

Chemim and I came to Canada to escape the political unrest where we lived in Meghalaya, a state in India. I had a degree in engineering. The Canadian government had accepted my licence, so we travelled here with high hopes. But it seemed that for the province of Ontario, all degrees are not created equal. I was told I had to re-train, and the cost was more than we could afford. No matter, we had to start somewhere. I took a job as a taxi driver, and Chemim worked at a donut shop. It was upsetting to me to think of her standing for hours, smiling at white faces that didn't smile back at her. We put every penny we could in the bank. We did our best to be happy. We did not complain.

We rented a small apartment in a low-income neighbourhood on Gerrard Street in the city of Toronto. There were many people from our culture and for that we were grateful. But it was noisy and dirty, with none of the beauty of our home city of Shillong, and we had difficulty adjusting to the cold of the winters.

When Chemim became pregnant with Sugith, she told me that she would not under any circumstances raise our child in such a place. I concurred. By then we had just enough money to make a down payment on a small house in Etobicoke.

English is a funny language. The bank manager laughed the first time I said it, told me it was not pronounced EE-TWO-BEE-COKE, but EH-TOW-BE-CO, which rhymes with GO.

When Sugith went into kindergarten, my sister Nazneen had come over from India, and moved in with us. This was a blessing, and a curse. A curse because Chemim did not like her – though thankfully that has changed. A blessing because she brought extra money into the household. This money went straight to my education fund. Chemim took in sewing to earn extra money. We got by.

My wife was pregnant with Jaswinder when I received my diploma, and by the time Jaswinder was ready for school, I was earning good money. We bought a nice house in the city of Mississauga, and opened up a savings account for our children's education.

SUGITH

Jaswinder was always whining to Mom and Dad about my *freedoms.*

"How come Sugith can go downtown by himself when I cannot."

Our father took my side. "Because he is a boy. Plain and simple. End of conversation."

I spent my Saturdays in Yorkville. It has lots of cool stores and places to hang out and watch girls.

One rainy afternoon, I decided to catch a flick with this hot girl I was dating. Sandra was white, and my father had forbidden me to date white girls. *They do not understand our culture and it will break your mother's heart.* Things got pretty hot between us in the theatre, and all I could think about was finding a place where we could go afterwards. As we walked out on to the street, I had one arm around Sandra, rubbing her arm up and down and getting it as close to her breast as possible. My eyes were adjusting from the darkness to the daylight. So I couldn't really see in front of me when who did I run into? My weird little sister. Dressed in my clothes, with a baseball cap to cover her hair. I detached myself from Sandra, hoping to make it look like maybe we didn't know each other, then yanked the hat off her stupid little head. She danced up and down, trying to grab it from my hand, squawking, "Give it back, you creep!"

"Get out of here you freak! Get home before I tell Father. And put my jeans back. I wondered where they went."

"Go ahead, you stupid goon. And I'll tell Mom I saw you here with a white girl." The cocky look on her face made me want to slap her.

JAZZ

The following Saturday I changed locations and went to Cabbagetown. Once the hangout of drunks and hookers, the area was now nuevo trendy. I missed the posh streets of Yorkville, but couldn't risk another run-in with my brother.

This uneasy truce with Sugith went on for months until THE DAY.

I was in my room, minding my own business, experimenting with giving myself a well-hung look by stuffing socks into the front pocket of my new jockey briefs. The door was shut, but that didn't stop Sugith.

"Mom sent me to ask you what you wanted for lunch." His eyes fixated on my crotch. "Why are you wearing guys' underwear? And what the hell is that?"

"It's just a sock, for god's sakes. Just a rolled-up sock." Sugith grabbed me and shook me until my teeth started clacking.

"This is too freakin' much. I'm telling Dad."

AMARJIT

My den is my sanctuary. A place for quiet reflection. To watch the phases of the moon and the subtle changes in the sugar maple outside my window as the seasons change.

It was a rainy spring evening and I was meditating on the sounds of the outside world when my son, all six-foot two and one hundred and sixty pounds of him, slammed open the door.

"Dad, Jaswinder is weird. She's been stealing my clothes, and...I think she's like...totally flipping out."

The relationship between my son and my daughter has always been strained. Jaswinder seems to resent the time I spent with Sugith. And Sugith is jealous of the amount of time Chemim spends worrying over her daughter. Things were bound to come to a head.

I took a deep breath, trying to push away the feeling of unease that rose up in me when I thought of Jaswinder and her peculiar way of being in the world. But I love her, and felt the need to defend her.

"Enough, Sugith. I know you do not like your little sister, but we all have to have patience with others, especially those we do not like."

"No, Dad, you don't get it. She's a queer. A freak. You should hear what the kids in school say about her."

"I don't want to listen to tattletales."

"For god's sakes, Dad! She's wearing guys' underwear and shoving socks down the front of her pants to make her look like she has…you know."

Things that are said in anger cannot be unsaid. I knew I needed a few minutes to calm myself. "Thank you for telling me this news, Sugith. It is not good news, but I did need to hear it nonetheless. Please go upstairs and ask Jaswinder to come down to talk to me in thirty minutes' time."

JAZZ

Of course, I knew why he wanted to see me. Knew that Sugith had told him. Knew it would not be pretty.

"Sugith tells me you are putting socks in your underwear to make it look like you have a penis. Is that true?" I wasn't about to lie. "We have tried to be patient with you, Jaswinder. But this is going too far. Your mother and I hope you soon will understand that you cannot undo your fate, which is to live as the woman you are. Do you understand? You must never do such a thing again."

I understood. Note to self. Put a lock on my door.

22

The headboard of my bed became the outlet for my rage. Nighttime found me in my room, the door securely locked, playing the knife thrower against all those who were my enemy.

CHEMIM

On the day she agreed to wear a sari to her cousin's wedding, I thought that she had finally stopped fighting what nature intended her to be. I cried with relief. At last, my daughter was becoming a woman.

She was beautiful on the day she graduated from high school, wearing a simple but lovely skirt that I had made for her. I couldn't have been more proud.

Today, the day of her seventeenth birthday, I was sure all would be well.

Although she put on the boyish clothing she likes so much, she let me brush her long hair until it shone.

The house was decorated. The living room filled with family and friends. All there to celebrate our beautiful girl. Our Jaswinder. I thought it was a new beginning. It was not.

I will leave the door unlocked tonight, for surely she will come home.

TRANSPLANT: *to dig up and plant in another place*

The coffee shop is full. I order a latte. Change my mind. Who knows when I'll get more money. I must spend it slowly.

"I'll have a small coffee. Vanilla Hazelnut. Is Jacob in today?"

The server, a tall, thin young man with blue eyes and long hair tied back with a piece of leather, regards me suspiciously.

"Jacob quit yesterday." Darn. "Are you a friend of his? Because he owes me money."

"Do you know where I can find him?" A burst of laughter, high and shrill from the other side of the room. "Sorry. No." I pay for the coffee. Load it up with sugar and cream. Add a dash of cinnamon. Look for an empty seat.

"There's an empty seat here." An older man, well off by the look of him, gestures for me to approach.

"Do you know Jacob? The guy who used the work the counter? He's a friend. I have to find him."

"Sure I know Jacob. Sweet guy." He pats the seat beside him. "But no, I don't know where he's gone. Sure you don't want to sit?"

"No thanks."

I grab a top for my coffee. Circulate among the patrons. "Anyone know where I can find Jacob?" Lots of heads shaking. I head out the door. This is not how it was supposed to play out.

~

I have jumped off the diving board of my destiny into the deep end. I'm not a good swimmer, and somebody better throw me a lifeline quick. I'm running low on friends, so in my current situation, I'll take what I can find, even if it's in an alleyway with a homeless guy.

24

Jean-Paul is an Indian who currently calls the lane behind the coffee shop his home. Two large plastic garbage bags hold all his worldly possessions. He looks up, checks me over, and then invites me to sit down. I offer him the rest of my coffee. It's cold, and the cream is slightly curdled. He drinks it down. Smacks his lips. I reach in my pocket. Offer him dessert. A stick of Trident. I have clearly made his day.

After an hour of conversation about this and that – the weather, sports (about which I know nothing) and politics (about which I know even less) he reaches over and pats my hand.

"Go home. These streets are no place for you at night."

He is fifty, but looks seventy. His nose is covered in broken veins. Lines of sorrow are carved around his eyes. One of his front teeth is missing. The others are covered in film. I make a note to buy him a toothbrush.

I have nothing to lose so I tell him my story. Then wait. For the familiar look of disgust to cross his face. Instead a twinkling in his eyes.

"Back in the day before the white man came to North America, people like you were honoured."

"Why?"

"Because you know the ways of both men and women."

"Really?"

"We have a name for you. 'Two-spirited'."

Two-spirited. I like that.

Night falls. He takes me to a mission for men. Tells me to pull up my hoodie, keep my head down. Let him do the talking.

I'm tired, but I can't sleep for the snoring and the stink of unwashed bodies. I keep my coat tucked around me and stay close to Jean-Paul.

Up early. Lukewarm coffee. A stale bran muffin. Then back on the street.

I power up my phone. Hoping for a message. An apology. A plea to come home. Nothing.

I buy us fresh coffee, and sandwiches from the corner store that taste like cardboard with mayonnaise. Settle down on steps in front of the Second Cup. Eyes scanning the street. Still hoping for a sign of Jacob.

"Tobacco is sacred to our people." Jean-Paul liked to smoke. Fascinating to watch him talk with a cigarette hanging out the side of his mouth, while his yellowed fingers are busy rolling another.

"Another thing you should know. We are called Indians because Columbus thought he had landed in India when he came to the shores of North America." A bit of history I wasn't familiar with. "So the truth is, you are an Indian and I am not. I am from the Cree Nation. From Manitoba. The Great Spirit speaks to me when the moon is full."

A police car drives by, slows to look, then drives on.

Three days away from home and I am learning things. First. The good people at the Second Cup don't like homeless Indians sitting on the stairs outside their establishment. The tall, thin young man with the ponytail doesn't make eye-contact when he shoos us away. Second. The human body gets smelly fast. Man, do I need a shower. Third. Restaurant owners don't let smelly people use their bathroom.

With nothing to do except hang out with Jean-Paul, there's lots of time to sit and think. Human nature is funny. Easy to make things black and white. Judge people as all good or all bad. I guess everyone is someone's freak. If I'd seen Jean-Paul on a shopping trip downtown with my mother, I would have turned away, repulsed by his greasy hair, the odour of tobacco and urine that clung to his clothes, the stink of sorrow. I would never have talked to him. Felt his kindness. Seen his nobility.

In just a few days, Jean-Paul has become a father figure of sorts. Making sure I eat by taking me to community soup kitchens. Making sure I have a bed at night. Alerting me to predators. On the morning of the third day away from home, with only two bars of battery remaining on my phone, and no messages, he kicks me out of the nest.

"It is not your destiny to live on the street. You do not belong here. I know someone who can help you. She's an ex-nun. Sister Mary Francis. Don't turn your nose up. She's good people."

As a parting gift, I take him out to the Korean barbeque for lunch. Leaves me with just over eighty dollars. We share the last of the Trident.

He gives me directions.

"Go down to Queen Street and take the streetcar west. Go to the community centre beside the church. It's on the south side. Somewhere around Logan. You've gone too far if you go across the river and under the sign that says 'You can't step in the same river twice'."

"Is that true?"

"I don't know. Ask Heraclitus."

"Who is Heraclitus?"

"An amazing Greek guy. You should look him up."

I walk south chewing my gum. Moving towards my destiny a little wiser, and with minty breath.

My mother took me twice a year to the dentist, once a year to the doctor, and once every two years to the optometrist. Into upscale buildings with spacious lobbies, easy-to-read signs directing you to your chosen medical professional, gleaming elevators, which moved silently and swiftly up and down. Beacons of professional respectability.

Which is why I do a triple take in front of the community centre. A dilapidated building, two stories high. Old brick covered with graffiti. Crumbling cement steps.

With dandelions, crabgrass and plantain poking up through the cracks.

I push through the heavy glass door into the foyer. No air conditioning. Smell of mold. Burned coffee. A big sign that says, *Ask and ye shall receive. Knock and the door will be opened unto ye.*

The furniture belongs to the last century. Goodwill castoffs. A few easy chairs with cushions. A stained orange couch. Dark wood paneling. Indoor/outdoor carpeting. One window. Surprisingly tidy.

I am met by a sea of eyes, all curious. One old woman stands. Waves at me. A little girl waves. Shuffles towards me in rubber boots two sizes too big. Big smile. No teeth. She takes my hand. Walks me over to the food table. Offers me a package of Dad's cookies. Pours me a cup of coffee.

"Twy it. Ith good." It isn't. But it's a nice gesture. She introduces me around. "Thith is Dorothy. Jim. Thuthan. Donna. Louith. Thamantha. And I'm Thinthia." Cynthia. I thank her. Take a seat. I hope there isn't a test later.

An orange-haired lady walks briskly towards me, slicing her hand up from her side to take mine in hers and welcome me to the centre.

"How can we help you today?"

How much do I say? Earth to self. Just talk to the woman. I clear my throat.

"My name is Jaswin...Jazz. I've come to see the social worker. The ex-nun? A friend of mine told me..." I start to babble.

She is clearly used to such discomfort. "Follow me, please." Her desk sits behind a grey room divider. She gestures to the yellow plastic chair beside her desk. Trying to put me at ease, she starts off with small talk. I sip and munch.

"Do you want to tell me why you are here?"

"I'd rather just talk to the social worker."

"I totally understand." Does she? I'm not quite sure how she could, but I'm grateful for the reprieve.

"I can make you an appointment for tomorrow afternoon."

"I need to see her today."

"Well, normally you have to have an appointment, but let me see what we have here." She flips open the appointment book. Looks at the clock. Tells me to wait right where I am until she gets back.

"You're in luck. Normally we don't take walk-ins, but we've just had a cancellation. Fill out this form and help yourself to some more coffee and cookies. The washrooms are down the hall. I'll let her know you are here."

The coffee tastes bitter. But it's free. No cream or milk. Just powdered creamer. Mixed with three teaspoons of white sugar, it's not so bad. I slip two packages of Dad's cookies in my jacket pocket. For later.

Revived by caffeine and sugar, I start in on the form. The first page is basic stuff. Name. Jazz Gupta. Address. The streets. Phone. My cell. Employed. No. I added three years to my age. Scribbled in my Medicare number. My medical history as best I could remember it. Reason for your visit? To be discussed.

Another swig of coffee. This stuff grows on you. I turn the page. Hold up. These are pretty personal questions. Had I experienced any early childhood trauma? Was I sexually active? If so, in a committed relationship or with multiple partners? Had I ever suffered from depression? Been diagnosed with a mental illness? Been hospitalized? Had I ever tried to commit suicide? To all of them I answer – none of your business. Then scratch it out. Better to leave it blank.

"She'll see you now. Down the hall to the left."

I refresh my coffee. I'm starting to get the shakes, but I'm enjoying the buzz. Walk down the long hall. Sean Penn in *Dead Man Walking*. I hope the ex-nun looks like Susan Sarandon. I stop in front of the only open door.

The office looks like a bomb has gone off. Scattered papers everywhere. Empty cans of Dr. Pepper. Half-eaten bags of chips. Boxes filled and overflowing with an assortment of this and that – file folders, office supplies, boxes of condoms.

In the centre of it all sits an old woman typing furiously on an outdated laptop. A laborious two-fingered peck that has her cursing under her breath. Shoulder-length gray hair. John Lennon granny glasses. A navy blue man's jacket with a white t-shirt underneath. The room is cramped. Stuffy. The walls covered by posters. Nature shots with inspirational messages.

A shot of Mount Fuji. *Believe in your dreams.*

A man with no legs competing in the Para-Olympics. *Courage plus persistence equals success.*

Some white bread motivational speaker supposedly inspiring an audience. *Insanity is doing the same thing over and over again and expecting a different result.*

Clichés. The slurry of Korean barbeque, bad coffee and Dad's cookies is not sitting well in my stomach. I wonder if they have any mint tea.

Oblivious of me, she taps the backspace button. Hits it harder. Then harder again. And again. Now shouting, "I didn't ask you to do that!"

I knock.

"Excuse me. Are you…?"

I've frightened her. She starts. Jerks her head up.

It's worse than I thought. She's really old. At least ninety. Her hair is exploded right out of the side of her head, like she just stuck her finger in an electric socket. Her glasses are taped on one side and sit crookedly on a face that looks permanently sunburned.

"Sorry. Please, come in and take a seat. I'll just be a minute."

Hand on the mouse, she clicks it once. Twice. Closes it down. Swivels her chair in my direction.

"I hate computers. What can I do for you?"

Holding out the vain hope that the gravelly-voiced woman in front of me is not the ex-nun, but her assistant, I say, "I'm here to see the social worker."

"You're looking at her."

"Really. You don't look like…"

"What? A social worker?"

"No. A nun."

"Very observant of you. I've made it a habit to not wear a habit."

She laughs. Slaps her thigh. Oh no. One of these people who does stand-up on amateur night at Yuk-Yuk's Comedy Club. This is not getting off to a good start.

She stares at me. Raises her eyebrows. Waiting for me to laugh. Sighs. Roots around in the top drawer of her desk. Pulls out a packet of Nicorette. Crams two pieces in her mouth.

"It's hell to quit smoking. Take it from me and never start. Now, tell me why you are here?"

SISTER MARY FRANCIS

Sullen. That is the word I would use to describe Jazz the first time he came to me. Sullen with a healthy dose of middle-class entitlement. And terrified. He didn't say that, of course. He didn't have to. It bled from his pores, the stains under the armpits of his cotton t-shirt the evidence of his terror.

He stands in my doorway, coffee in hand, a look of bored indifference on his face, a dirty windbreaker tied around his waist.

"I'm here to see the social worker. When will she be here?" I am obviously not what he had in mind.

He stares at me, and I stare at him, a pissing contest to see who would be dominant. I win.

He sits in the armchair across from me as if he might be sitting in dog poop. Granted, it did have a big brown stain on it. But it was just coffee. The chair came from my mother's estate. That and a box of bone china were all I had left from my family of origin. When he starts picking at the stuffing poking up from the armrest, I make a mental note to tape it.

I pick up his intake form. Twenty years old. I look back up. Study his face. Hell, if he's twenty, I'm a size 5. No address listed. Not good. Neat handwriting on page one. Angry scratching on page two.

Sitting back in my office chair, I note the growing pile of stuffing from my mother's armchair on his knee. I also note his expensive designer jeans and t-shirt, both slightly worse for the wear. There is a ketchup stain on the front. Probably recent. His fingernails are dirty, and his short black hair longer on one side than the other. A fashion choice?

"There's no address listed here. Where are you living?"

"I'm fine."

"Glad to hear you're fine, but I need the address please."

"I...live with a friend."

He swirls the last of his coffee in the Styrofoam cup. Drinks it down. Swivels in the chair, throwing one long leg over the armrest. The picture of bored nonchalance.

"It says here your name is Jazz Gupta. Is that correct?"

"Correct."

"Jazz. That's an interesting name. Is it short for something?"

"No."

"How can I help you?"

"Dunno."

"So far I'm impressed with your ability to answer every question mono-syllabically, but can we focus in and get to the reason why you came to see me. Why are you here?"

Silence.

"In case you are concerned, everything you say in this

room stays in this room. In other words, it's confidential. So speak now or let me get back to my work."

"I need some help." He's struggling. I nod my head. The social worker's non-verbal show of listening. "I need to find out more about…" Keep nodding. You can do it. Spit it out.

"I'm transgendered." He looks at me as if he expects me to be shocked. Pulls out a handful of stuffing from the armrest. Stares at the floor.

"I can see that was hard. And good for you having the courage to reach out for help."

"Jean-Paul said you were a good person."

Ah, gee. Nice to know I'm well regarded amongst the homeless. "How is Jean-Paul?"

"Good."

"Would you be able to…I need to…why is this so freaking hard?"

"Because it just is. That's why. Care for a Dr. Pepper?"

"Sure." I toss one his way. He catches it. Cracks it open. Soda fizzes up and out and onto his shirt.

"Shit!"

"Hey, no one gets to swear in here but me." I laugh and hand him a towel.

He wipes his shirt. Takes a big slurp. Covers his mouth. Burps. Apologizes. "I need you to help me…you know…really be a man."

"Honey, you are either a man or you are not. There are lots of human beings walking around with penises that are about as far away from being a man as our Prime Minister is from being honourable. Care for some potato chips?"

"No thanks."

I munch as we talk. "Do you have a job?"

"Not yet. But I'll get one."

"Do you have any money?"

"Yeah, sure."

"How much?"

"Enough."

"Are your parents alive?"

"Yes."

"Will they help you?"

"Only if I'll put on a sari and marry the man of their dreams."

I crack up. I'm beginning to like this kid.

He is telling me his story – a great leap of trust I know – when the phone rings.

"Glenna, I'm in a session….What?... Oh, no. Not again…I'll be there in a minute." I hang up the phone.

"I'm sorry, Jazz, but I need to wrap up our session. I have to go to the police station to pick up a client." Jerry is a schizophrenic who occasionally goes off his meds and gets into fights. Sometimes it's not too bad. This time he lost all his front teeth. Thank God welfare covers emergency dental work.

He jerks his head up. Crosses his arms over his chest. Flares his nostrils. If he'd started pounding his hooves on the floor and bellowing I wouldn't have been surprised. Hell's bells. Do we have to have another pissing contest?

"Is that it? We're done? I don't have time to screw around, lady. Is there someone else I can talk to?"

Perfect segue. "Yes, in fact there is. I'm going to refer you to a counselor up at the 519. Come back tomorrow and we'll get you set up."

JAZZ

I hate her right now. Hate how easy it was for her to brush me off.

She's in a hurry. Talking fast. "Speak to Glenna on your way out. Tell her I said I need to see you first thing tomorrow."

"Who is Glenna?"

"You talked to her when you came in?" Oh right. Carrot top.

"How long?"

She's grabbing her purse. Checking for her keys. "Excuse me?"

"How long until this guy…what's his name?"

"Kendall Johnson."

"How long until this Kendall Johnson can see me?"

"As I said, I'll know more when you come back tomorrow."

What am I supposed to do between now and tomorrow morning?

What a waste of time. To hell with her.

I hit the bathroom. Pee. Wash my hands. My face. Fill up my water bottle. *Where am I going to sleep tonight?* I look for a window – a place to crawl in from the outside. No go. The windows are old and painted shut. I power on my phone. Check for messages. Nothing. Only one bar of power left.

I slide down to cool tile floor. It's dirty. But then so am I. *Don't make decisions when you are hungry, angry, tired or lonely.* That was one of my mother's maxims. Right now I am all four of these things.

I have to make a decision.

I can go back to Jean-Paul.

Join the circus.

Or kill myself.

Suicide. Not really my style. But…imagine.

The call to Sister Mary. *Your client has offed himself in the washroom.* She enters. Sees my blood spattered on the wall. My eyes lifeless. Staring. She has a coronary. Drops dead.

Or better yet. I walk up to my parents' home. Calm. Collected. Ring the doorbell. They open it. Look angry. Then, heartbroken, when they see my derelict state. As they reach out their arms to embrace me, my last words. *I am your child, and yet you want me only if I am willing to betray myself. You are so filled with hate and judgment that you leave me no choice. Let it be said that you are parents who have killed their son.*

I pull out a gun. Boom. Blow my head off. Splattering them with blood and a lifetime of guilt. Righteous.

Out the heavy front door and into the late afternoon sun. It's almost dinnertime. From the open windows of restaurants, smells of food cooking. My mouth starts to water. A happy couple sits under an umbrella in a sidewalk cafe, drinking cold lemonade. I slug back some water. It's warm. Not exactly refreshing. I decide to save my last token and walk back to Church and Wellesley. Find Jean-Paul. Tell him the whole sad tale.

He's nowhere to be found. Not on the street. In the bathroom at the library. In his favourite alleyway.

I flop in the parkette on the corner of Maitland and Church to consider my options. Nothing and nothing.

Across the street. Kim's Kutz. A sign on the window. Help wanted. What the hell? Why not.

At the front desk is a woman with long blonde hair and shoulders the size of a football player. "Can I help you?"

I look around. Hot pink window curtains. Gaudy art deco furniture. Turquoise floor rugs. A mural covers one wall. Freddy Mercury. Before he cut his hair. Cradling the microphone. The conduit that carries his soul song. *We are the champions!*

"I'm here about the job."

The receptionist flips her hair back from her face in one elegant, practiced gesture. Turns. Drops her voice an octave and she shouts into the back of the salon. "Kimmie! It's someone about the job."

Despite the law that says that there will be no smoking in public places. Kimmie waves a cigarillo theatrically into the air, leaving a trail of smoke in its wake as he sails up to the front desk. He is my height. Anorexically thin. Purple hair like a rooster's comb sticking straight up from his head. He meets my eyes straight on. I suddenly realize how I must look. And smell.

"I'm here about the job."

"Résumé?"

"I don't have one."

"References?"

I stammer. "I…I…"

"I know. You don't have that either. Ever worked in a salon before?"

"No."

"Don't have much to recommend you, do you?" He arches his finely tweezed eyebrows. Takes a drag from his cigarillo.

I gird myself for the inevitable rejection. Hold my head up. Take charge. "Smoking in public places is illegal, you know."

The receptionist places her large bejeweled hand over her cherry plum painted lips. Gasps. Faux shock. Winks at Kimmie. Who winks at her before turning stern eyes to me.

"This is not a public place. It is my place, smartass." Why is everyone calling me that? "I think this interview is over. Delores, show this obnoxious little boy out."

It's not lost on me. That he called me boy. Not girl.

"Wait. I'm sorry."

He doesn't miss a beat. "You should be."

"I really need a job. I'll do whatever it takes. I'm smart. I learn fast. Please."

A pause. Then another. How long will he make me stand here?

"How old are you?"

"Twenty-one." I'm getting older by the minute.

"Really? Can I see your I.D.?"

"I left it at home."

"I thought so. Delores, I need a coffee. Would you like a coffee…what's your name?"

"Jazz. And I'd prefer a mint tea."

"A mint tea? Oh la dee da. Tea and a cappuccino. Take the cash from the register." He points to the back of the salon. Freddy Mercury sings encouragement in my ear. *We are the champions of the world.*

"If you are going to work here, you have to learn how to wash hair. I'll demonstrate on you. Watch and learn." Like a magician before his best trick, he snaps open the plastic cape, then twirls it over my shoulders. Grandly, he gestures towards the turquoise leather chair. Then not so gently pulls my head back. Turns on the water.

"Honey, when is the last time you washed this hair?" I close my eyes. Let go into the sensation of warm water on my head, his fingers on my scalp. The smell of apricot shampoo. Apple conditioner. It's over all too soon.

He sits me up. Towel dries my hair with a fluffy white towel that smells like Downy. Drapes the towel neatly around my shoulders. Takes my hand and leads me over to a chair.

Delores returns with the coffee and my tea. I stir in three sugars. Sip as he pulls the comb over my clean scalp.

"Who is responsible for this hack job on your hair?"

"I am."

"Remind me not to let you near the scissors."

With my hair clean, I feel better than I've felt in days.

"Take this." He hands me a pink t-shirt with the Kim's Kutz logo on the front and back. "There's a bathroom in the back. Wash as much of you as you can, and put this on."

In the poorly lit bathroom, I strip off my top. Do my best to scrub the dirt from my face and hands, the stink from my armpits.

Back in the salon, Kimmie wastes no time. Shoves a broom in my hand.

"You're on trial for the rest of the day. We close at seven, so you have two hours to show me that I haven't made a huge mistake. Keep the floors and counters clean. And stay out of my way."

By 7:20, the shop is empty. I have swept the parquet floor so that not a hair remains. I have wiped the counters down, polishing them until they shine. I have thrown away all used coffee cups, emptied Kimmie's ashtray, and loaded the washing machine with the dirty towels.

Kimmie looks about. Nods his approval. "The job pays minimum wage and not a penny more. You get a 20% discount on all products and services. Your hours are Tuesday to Saturday from 9:30-7:30 with one hour for lunch and two fifteen-minute breaks. No overtime. Sorry. We're not a union shop." I thank him. Try not to grovel. "One more thing. Don't come tomorrow without taking a shower. 'Cause I got to tell you, boy...you stink. No insult intended."

"None taken." The problem of where to sleep jumps up. Grabs me by the throat. *Think.* Maybe I can probably get a cheap hotel room somewhere on the outskirts of the city? "Any chance you could pay me for the work I did today? And maybe advance me a bit?"

Months later Kim would tell me that he knew then. Knew I was homeless. And clueless.

"I don't know why I'm doing this, but I know a queer in trouble when I see one."

"I'm not..."

Kim waves his hand, brushing my protests away. "There's a cot in the back. You can sleep there tonight. Here's what you earned today. Go out, get something to eat, and meet me back here. I'm upstairs. Just press the buzzer."

I feel like I've won the lottery. Hit the jackpot. I have

hope for the first time since I left home. Surging, soaring hope. A job. Access to a shower. A place to sleep.

"Hey!" A voice from across the street. "Hey! You!"

"Me?"

"Yah, you in the pink t-shirt." J-walking across the street. Two young rednecks. Plaid shirts. Low slung jeans. Greasy hair. Cigarettes dangling from their lips. A backwoods cliché.

The taller of the two has hair the colour of beets. He stops in front of me. Sneers.

"What are you anyway? A boy or a girl?"

"What are you? A jerk or an idiot?"

He hangs his thumbs on his belt. O.K. Corral style. He's up for a shoot-out and I've left my pistols at home.

A car shrieks to a stop in the middle of the road. A gold Impala. Rusted out with balding tires. The driver, another redneck, leans his head out the window, yelling.

"Donny! Come on! I got to get this car back."

The other guy, the not-Donny, looks around. "We're coming." Grabs his friend. Pulls him towards the curb.

Donny yanks his arm away. Is not so easily rushed. "I got somethin' to finish here first." He forgot to add Pardner.

This is where we turn. Walk back twenty paces. Whip around and shoot. Pow, pow, pow.

Cars are backing up behind the Impala. Slow crescendo of horns. A male voice shouts, "Move it, asshole."

The driver pounds the outside of the door with his hand.

"Donny. Norman. Come on, you jerks."

I laugh. Spit the words up into his smug face. "Hey, I was right. You're a jerk."

Mezzo forte honking. A chorus of voices raised in anger at the driver of the Impala. Norman inserts himself between Donny and me. Nose to nose. Donny and Norman.

"Donny, stop being an asshole and leave him...her... whatever the fuck it is, and let's go."

40

Donny, who must have the last laugh, throws back his head. Spits on the sidewalk. Slams his fist into my shoulder. Knocks me back. "Later, queer boy."

I look around to see who was watching. Nobody.

As I head up the street, I admit to myself that I thought I would crap my pants.

SISTER MARY

It's Monday. Four days since he came to see me, and not a word. I sip my green tea. Try to ignore the gnawing feeling in my gut that I missed an important clue. That I should have let Jerry wait and given him just a bit more time. I close my eyes. Say a prayer that this kid is not in an alleyway somewhere beat up or turning tricks.

But at ten o'clock, he shows up pretty as you please. Clean clothes. Clean hair. A pretty pink t-shirt. Waltzes past Glenna and into my office as if he owned the place. I shake my head. First with relief. Then with anger. I want to say...*I'm busy. You'll have to make an appointment with Glenna, just like everyone else.* But professional courtesy gets the better of me.

"Jazz. I was worried. I'm glad to see you are okay."

"I got a job."

"Good for you."

"Did you set up a time for me to meet with that guy from the 519?"

"Yup. It was for Friday at two o'clock. You missed it." His face falls. Then opens like a book to a chapter called Please Help Me. I let it sink in.

"I had to work on Friday."

"Never heard of the telephone?" Maybe his mother let him get away with this crap, but I wasn't about to. I let him stew in his own juices for a minute.

"Sorry."

"Thanks. So, how's it going? At your new job, that is."

"I'm starting as a sweeper at a hair salon up on Church Street. You've probably never heard of it. Kim's Kutz."

"I know."

"How'd you know?"

"Firstly, you're wearing the company t-shirt. Second, I live just up the road from Kim. He's a friend. From the look on his face, I might as well have told him that the Pope was gay. "Not a close friend. But we do coffee from time to time." I was stretching the truth. I knew Kim from years ago when he was working for the AIDS Committee. I hadn't seen him in years. I'll have to give him a call. Grease the wheel of connection.

"Just give me a minute. I'll call Ken. See what I can set up."

Relieved, he settles back in his chair, looks around. Along the left side of his head, I notice streaks of turquoise, pink and white. A trans rainbow. Nice.

Things I remember about being a girl. Starched skirts. Itchy crinolines. Black patent leather shoes that pinched. Easter bonnets. Caroling at Christmas. Eating too many desserts at church suppers. Running in fields of tall grass. Picking daisies. Squishing spiders. My Grandmother's mashed potatoes. My mother's stern hand. My father. Happy by day. Drunk by night. His big hands pawing me through my pajamas.

I never wanted to be a boy. But there were lots of things I didn't like about being a girl. *Be nice. Smile. Talk softly. Don't stare. Don't be a know-it-all. Don't laugh so loud. Sit with your legs closed. You are what you look like. He didn't mean to hurt you.*

Raised at the end of an era that is thankfully over, when I graduated high school my mother gave me three options. Get married and have children. Become a nurse, then get married and have children. Become a nun. I chose the third. Not because I felt any particular calling, but because I needed a way out of the house.

It wasn't bad at first. Good food. A predictable routine. Up early. Pray. Eat. Work. Pray. More work. More praying. Sleep. Then get up and do it all again. No one told me I couldn't be as smart as I am (though I was censured many times for my smart mouth). No one came in my room at night.

My dream was to be a doctor. To travel to other countries and do missionary work. Instead I was sent to earn a degree as a teacher, then sent to teach in a local Catholic school. It was not what I wanted, but personal choice is not front and centre when decisions are made in the convent.

My father died when I was forty. I didn't go home. But I prayed for him in the chapel by day. Cursed his soul to hell at night in my cell. My mother took sick two days after my fifty-fifth birthday. Cancer of the liver. I was released from my duties, and came back to Toronto to take care of her.

The outside world had changed a great deal. It was at the height of the AIDS crisis. Young men dropping like flies, dying unspeakably horrible deaths.

But more horrible still was public response to it, spearheaded by the Church. AIDS as a judgment from God. A punishment for sin.

My mother – God bless her – took up the cause, her anger a clarion call to the bigots in her church. She held prayer meetings – first in our home, and later in her room at St. Margaret's hospital. Rosary beads in hand, the ladies prayed to the Blessed Virgin for the poor and the sick, the sinners who had lost their way, and the Pope and his ministers on earth. Washing their sanctity down with strong tea and sugary cake, they then allowed themselves a few minutes of outraged whispering about the *gay problem*.

My mother was allowed an extra slice of bile. She was dying after all. *Filthy faggots.* In the end, I'm not sure what actually killed her. The cancer or the hate.

I sold her house, paid her debts and gave the rest of the money to the AIDS Committee of Toronto, a dynamic group of impassioned people working to make a difference.

I went back to the convent. Told the Mother Superior I wanted to go out into the community and work with AIDS patients. My request was denied. That didn't sit well with me. Wasn't I supposed to be serving the God of love?

I asked her to petition Rome on my behalf. To be released from my vows. She didn't like it. But she had no choice.

With the help of a student loan, I received my Masters in Social Work in my sixtieth year.

I'll be seventy-two this November. I live in a small bungalow with my dog, Emma. It's not far from where I work. I am saving my money to visit Thailand, and I eat a lot of Chinese take-out. I love my life.

Psychologically, I still think of myself as a nun. And I still call myself Sister.

I received a letter last year from Rome, threatening to excommunicate me if I continue to call myself Sister. I say, bring it on.

"If you hustle up there right now, Ken can see you before lunch."

"And he'll help me?"

"He's a brilliant man. Transgender. Just like you."

KENDALL

I like playing with the sounds of words.

Caroling. Cacophony. Chorus.
Kill. Crisis. Crucify.
Serendipity. Stupor. Super Nova.
Perceive. Deceive. Deliverance.

The etymology of words fascinates me. Take for instance the words *freak* and *weird*.

FREAK: *1560s, "sudden turn of mind," of unknown origin, perhaps related to Old English* frician, *"to dance."*

WEIRD: *c.1400, "having power to control fate, from* wierd *(n.), from Old English* wyrd.*"*

Both of these words have often been used as pejorative labels. And yet, the etymology of the words tells a different story, which allows for a very different personal response. Turning a barb into a boon, so to speak.

So much so, that when, from a state of outright ignorance, another human being calls me one of these names, I affirm loudly. *Yes, I am indeed weird and a freak, and thank-you for your astute observation. Have a wonderful day.*

I tell this to my clients to make them laugh, but more so to make them think.

I am fascinated by patterns. Patterns in history. Patterns in nature. Patterns of human behaviour. Patterns of pain visited by humans on humans generation after generation. Xenophobia in different guises.

It was illegal to be anything other than a regular heterosexual when I was young, so I tried to hide my state of gender confusion from both myself and the world at large. Following the natural sexual urges of a sixteen-year-old, I pursued a beautiful young woman named Audrey. Privately and away from prying eyes, over the course of a summer, Audrey let me walk with her, then hold her hand, then kiss her.

But when it was time to go back to school, something changed. Poor Audrey. She got scared, I guess. She told her brother about our clandestine meetings. James, doing what a good brother does when his sister is threatened, called me a freak (note the use of the word), beat the crap out of me and broke my nose. Though my father took me to the doctor to have my nose set, he didn't ask a single question about what happened. I believe that he considered me a kind of freak as well.

When I was eighteen, Eddy – who was literally the boy next door – asked me to marry him. I said yes because I knew I should, but in the end, I got cold feet, realizing I couldn't play-act the whole fall-in-love-get-married-thing. I moved away and got a job at a canning factory for the summer, where I saw things that turned me off ever eating canned vegetables again. When I had saved enough money, I went to university to study biology. I wanted to learn why the sky is blue, how the tides turn, what makes the grass such a verdant green in spring, and why nature made me the way I am.

In school, I learned that nature loves biodiversity. For example, we think of gender in very black and white terms, hence the social prejudice towards people who are alternately gendered (there were no such politically correct terms in my young days, only pejoratives like queer, fag, freak, lesbo). However in nature, we see that many natural organisms do not retain their birth sex. Many plants have both sexes and fertilize themselves. In some animal species, females have the same chromosomes as males. Female spotted hyenas have penis-like structures identical to males. The male fruit bat has milk-producing mammary glands. When the dominant female clownfish dies, a male can take over and be capable of breeding.

In university, I shared a dorm room with Suzanne, who was also a science major. Women in the field of science were few and far between in those days, so we stuck together, even though she thought I was a bit weird (note word usage).

We walked through campus together, for camaraderie as well as protection from the groups of male students who travelled in packs and didn't like it that we had inserted ourselves into their male-only club. They would often approach us on the street or in the cafeteria to razz us, and when they couldn't get a rise out of us, the rant would deteriorate, and, spitting and cursing, they would have the last word.

"Bitches!"

I would smile, then spit out my witty retort. "A bitch

is a female dog. Your eyesight must be failing." It felt good at the time, but in hindsight, it was probably not the wisest thing to do.

In second year, I opened up to Suzanne about myself, my history and my quandary about what I was. She couldn't wrap her head around it. Very few people could in those days.

"I don't get it. You're attracted to women. Why don't you just call yourself a lesbian?"

"Why don't you just call yourself a tomato?"

After years of referring to myself as androgynous, by the time I graduated, I was relatively comfortable with the term *transgender*. However, in the dominant culture, it was still an anomaly. Then, in 1999, the movie *Boys Don't Cry* came out in the theatres. It was based on a true story of Brandon Teena, who identified and passed as male until she was found out and murdered. For her brilliant portrayal of Brandon Teena, Hilary Swank not only won an Oscar, she also gave a voice to those of us who had previously been voiceless, a name to those who had previously been nameless.

The ex-nun from the community centre in Riverdale is sending me a young transgendered male with some kind of musical name. I am hoping he does not identify as Christian. They burned too many of us.

JAZZ

Kendall is trying really hard to help me. And I am trying really hard to like him. I should like him. Right? I mean, how many other transgender guys have I met? But the truth is, he creeps me out. If this is my future, I'm not sure I want to go there. He is exactly what I don't want to be. An aging, semi-balding transman with a big belly and tufts of facial hair growing in random patches on his face. He also has a crooked nose and sweats like a pig. A classic academic, he talks in long sentences and delights in using big words. He has been talking non-stop since I got here, and now is staring at me with his big owl eyes.

"I'm sorry. Did you ask me a question?"

The one thing I have to give him is this. He's a very classy dresser. Linen dress pants. Which lie perfectly tailored on his Gucci leather boots. Colour-coordinated with his cream-coloured linen jacket. Very GQ. My mother would like him for that.

"I want to get started on..." He chimed in. Upbeat. A pep talk he'd given a hundred times before.

"Your transition. You want to start your transition. Is that what you mean?"

"I've done the research. I want to do the whole thing."

"What whole thing would that be?" His owl eyes are blinking rapidly. Why is he making me say it? "If it's hard for you to say, you may find that it even harder to do. Tell me, Jazz. What are you feeling right now?" His owl eyes are open wide. Expectant.

"Uh, I don't know. Good. Frustrated."

"Are you frightened?"

"Hell, no."

I look at his chest. Wondering. I think it's probably too soon to ask, but I risk it. "Have you had the surgery?"

He shifts in his chair. Clears his throat. Pushes the cuticle back on his left ring finger.

"Don't you find it curious?"

"What?"

Big sigh. "Never mind."

He reaches into his top drawer. Pulls out a brochure. Opens it so I can read it. Takes a red marker and circles a listing for a support group.

"I'm going to suggest that you join our support group.

This will give you a chance to meet other transgender people, which I believe will help you feel less isolated."

"I didn't say I feel isolated."

"We meet every other Monday night starting at seven, which means you can start tonight if you want. We provide healthy snacks, and money for transit if you need it."

"I don't want to join a support group. I don't want to talk about how I feel. I want to get going. Testosterone. Surgery."

He hands me a pamphlet. "Read this. It will give us a place to start." I look at the pamphlet in my hand. *Transgender 101. All you need to know to live your true identity.* Then he turns to his bookshelf. Pulls a fat book off the shelf.

"Because you are so keen to know about the holy grail of gender re-assignment, here's a book complete with pictures. I'll be back in a few minutes. Take a look."

Now we're talking. I flip it open. Scan down the index to chapter four and find what I'm looking for.

TRANSITIONING MEDICALLY F2M

HORMONE THERAPY

Testosterone, also known as T., is the hormone used in transgender males who desire to exhibit the physical attributes of a biological male. When you begin your hormone therapy, you will essentially be entering a second puberty. T. It can be injected or applied dermally. When it reaches the level present in a biological male, the following will occur: Menstruation will cease. Increase in body and facial hair (may take up to several years and may be accompanied by male pattern baldness). Voice lowers (though not in all cases). Higher libido. Enlarged clitoris. Increase in lean muscle mass. Body fat will re-distribute. Acne and oily skin is a common side effect. Also sterility.

At the bottom of the page is a picture of Dan, a young transman who has been undergoing testosterone therapy for four years. His beard is in, his upper body is bulked up and he looks happy. That will be me.

GENDER REASSIGNMENT SURGERY

Since gender re-assignment surgeries are rarely covered by health insurance. Be prepared to undertake a substantial financial commitment both for the surgical procedures and for convalescent time.

CHEST OR TOP SURGERY

Patients undergo a double-incision mastectomy to remove breast tissue. The nipples are re-sized and shaped and sewn back onto the chest wall. This is considered a major surgery.

Shown is a picture of Dan with a hairy chest. A large scar loops like a handlebar mustache across his chest from armpit to armpit. Not so bad.

BOTTOM OR LOWER SURGERY.

Less common among F2Ms due to high risk of complications. There are two options.

Medioplasty. During this procedure the clitoris is released. This, along with testosterone therapy can give the clitoris the appearance of a small penis. The urethra can be extended through the clitoris so that urination can happen from a standing position. The vagina can be permanently closed and a scrotum constructed out of the tissue. Testicular implants are then added.

Phalloplasty. During this procedure, a penis is constructed out of flaps of skin from various parts of the body. A complete phalloplasty includes multiple surgeries – as many as eight or nine – over a period of many months to a year. Nerves are connected to allow for sensation, but there is no guarantee that this will be successful. The urethra is routed through the newly constructed penis. It will take at least a year following the final surgery for the penis to have sensation. As in the medioplasty, the vagina can be sewn shut to allow for the creation of testicular implants and an erectile prosthesis can be added. The penis will be the size of a biological male. However, the prosthesis requires pumping to become erect. Sensation is limited to the head of the penis. The high risk of complications includes severe scarring, difficulty urinating and fistulas, along with a significant risk of never regaining sensation in the penis or donor sites. In a very few cases, the reconstructed penis has fallen off.

Three pictures. One of arms marked by the surgeon for the harvesting of large skin flaps to construct the penis. That looks painful. The next a picture of the testicular implants. They don't look too bad. And then the reconstructed penis. Which does look like a penis, but without the wrinkly skin. The thought of what goes into creating it makes me feel more than a bit squeamish. I repress a gag.

Ken is standing behind me, stirring sugar into his tea. "Quite a bit of slicing and dicing to get the desired affect, don't you think?" I'm trying not to.

"I know it will be hard, but I'm going to do it."

"It's also quite expensive."

"How much?"

"For the whole shebang? Top and bottom? Plus money to pay for the time you can't work as you heal? Maybe fifty thousand dollars."

"You're kidding. It can't be that much. You just don't want me to do this. Why are you trying to talk me out of it?" I notice for the first time that his right eye is different from his left eye. One sharp-looking. Cold. The other, veiled. Sad.

"I'm not. I just want you to get as much information as you can before you make a decision. There are lots of other routes to go. You should explore all your options."

"How many routes are there?"

"Lots."

TRANSITION: *a passing from one place, subject, or state to another*

Did I ever pull a lemon in the garden of counselors! I feel sick to my stomach. Slicing and dicing indeed. Is this what he calls support?

Despite the fact that I feel like decking him, I am going to attend the support group. I'd like to meet some other transgender people. And I could use some good snacks, and some friends.

There are five of us here, including Kendall, who directs us all to pull our chairs into a circle. We discuss the rules of confidentiality. How to listen. How to support. Why it is important to allow everyone to *be where they are at*.

I'm the new kid, so Kendall introduces me and gives me the floor. I try to make a joke.

"Hi. I'm Jazz. I'm transgendered and powerless to stop it." No one laughs except Karly.

Karly is a post-op transwoman who has hit rock bottom emotionally and financially. She is struggling with her demons and using alcohol to self-medicate. She attended her first twelve-step meeting last night, which is why she laughed at my joke. Married thirty years to the same woman, his wife did not adjust well to life with her new female husband, even though she initially supported his transition. Neither did the kids, who are now all grown up with children of their own. She passes around pictures of her two grandsons, then breaks down as she tells us how she has never met them and probably never will. Kendall hands her a tissue.

"Why can't you meet them?" I blurt out. Clearly I'm the only one in the group that doesn't know.

"Because they don't want their kids to meet their freak grandfather." More sobs. Kendall moves in, rubs her back, and gives her another tissue.

"I cashed in my RRSPs to pay for my surgeries. And now, my wife wants a divorce." Kendall calls a bathroom break, then takes her hand and whispers something in her ear. She blows her nose. Smiles wanly. Then throws her arms around him and sobs some more. Poor Karly.

L.J. is about the closest in age to me. He's taller than me by an inch or two and has a great five o'clock shadow. His hips are wider than a normal guy's, but are offset by his upper body. He must lift a lot of weights. He is a successful singer/songwriter with his own band. He came out in the public eye, and thinks everyone else should too. He welcomes me to the group. I like him right off.

Next to him, hands fluttering about like a butterfly, constantly adjusting his/her sweater to cover the long scar that runs up the inside of his/her left arm, is Jaden. She sits somewhere on the gender spectrum but doesn't want to be labeled. Kendall reminds us that everyone should be free to identify themselves however they choose. Jaden likes to be referred to as *hir*. Fair enough. Jaden is six-foot tall with skin so pale hir could almost be albino. Light blue eyes, long neck and painfully skinny. Tonight hir is wearing a tailored man's suit along with make-up and heels. Hir has a wicked sense of humour, and has us all in stitches with tales of the escapades of her cat, Tabitha. Hir works in a travel agency and I can't help but wonder what pronoun they use for hir there. At the end of hir share, she clears her throat and quotes the poet Rumi.

"Run from what's comfortable. Forget safety. Live where you fear to live. Destroy your reputation. Be notorious."

After group, L.J. and I go for coffee at the Second Cup. I look for the gangly creep who kicked me off the steps last week, just so I can shoot him a dirty look. He's not there. L.J. is an activist to the core. I want to talk to him about his transition. He wants me to join a group of other F2Ms who are working *to educate society on the difference between sexuality and sexual identity. To raise awareness of the gender spectrum. To put an end to trans-related hate crime.* I tell him I'll think about it. But I know I won't. Right now, I don't want to be an activist. I just want to be a regular guy.

KENDALL

I was glad to see Jazz connect with L.J. at the meeting. He's a good guy, a bit of a zealot, but who can blame him. Three years into his transition, he's gone from turning tricks to having a successful musical career.

Jazz is definitely on the go-for-broke transition trail. At least for now. Ready and raring to go. During his next appointment I suggest a visit to the doctor.

"What for?"

"You'll need a referral to an endocrinologist if you want to start on T. Can you make an appointment with your family doctor?"

"Not about this."

I thought as much but I did have to ask. "Here's the number for Doctor Horowitz. He's new in the neighbourhood and is taking patients."

JAZZ

Dr. Horowitz is late. I pass the time by chatting to his receptionist, Martin, a self-described flaming queen.

It turns out that Martin has an apartment above a green grocer on Church Street, and he's looking for a roommate. He says he has a penchant for taking in lost souls, and when I tell him I'm looking for a place to stay, he swoons at the happy coincidence.

"It's a one and a half bedroom." He grabs a pen, sketches out the layout of the apartment on the back of a requisition form, then gestures around the waiting room, explaining that he decorated each and every inch of the office space.

The walls are a fleshy shade of peach and are covered in floral prints. Martin explains that "Pastels are known to inhibit violent or self-destructive impulses." I'm not sure why such impulses would occur in a G.P.'s office, but I don't ask.

Black leather chairs with metal armrests are bolted firmly to the floor. "So the patients not only sit in comfort, but will feel grounded."

The floor is covered in chocolate brown broadloom, and the shiny glass top table in the centre of the room is reserved for a giant crystal dish full of assorted candies. "For people with low blood sugar. Plus, it looks pretty." He giggles. He seems to have thought of everything. We hammer out a deal.

For $50 a week I will get the full run of the apartment, including phone and cable television. I won't have my own bedroom, but will have the pull-out couch, which sits in a small den, with a Chinese screen for privacy. Occasionally he may have to ask me to spend the night elsewhere if he needs the place to himself, but that will rarely need to happen. We shake hands. It's a win/win made in queer heaven.

I settle into one of the waiting room chairs, and the smell of new leather fills my nostrils. I pop a candy in my mouth, and enjoy the lemony zing. I pick up a copy of *National Geographic* and read about the loss of animal habitat in the Rainforest.

On display units on the wall are brochures artfully designed to grab the eye. They offer services for those in crisis, warn of the dangers of unprotected sex, explain why a tetanus shot is necessary if you garden with bare hands. On the corner table is one of those plug-in fountains that gurgles and spits when it runs low on water.

Out of the corner of my eye, I watch my new landlord. Martin is all business, answering phones, making appointments, tidying up the myriad of magazines and newspapers that Dr. Horowitz subscribes to. He pats my knee as he brushes by. Whispers in my ear, "At home you can call me Martine. We are going to be good friends. I can tell."

I'm in and out of Dr. H's office in a flash. Fresh out of medical school, he is fresh-faced and full of enthusiasm. A devout practitioner of Western Medicine, he is proud to be working in the front lines of the heart of Canada's gay rights movement.

"I've talked to Dr. Johnson at length about your case…" I want to interrupt him to ask who the heck is Dr. Johnson, and then I remember that Johnson is Kendall's last name. "…and I just need to confirm your diagnosis before we proceed with the referral." He reverently opens up his brand new copy of the *DSM-IV* – the bible of psychiatric medicine. He flips to a page he has marked with a bright purple sticky note, and reads aloud.

"Gender Identity Disorder.

1. A strong and persistent cross-gender identification (not merely a desire for any perceived cultural advantage of being the other sex).

2. Persistent discomfort with his or her sex or sense of inappropriateness in the gender role of that sex.

"Does this seem to describe your current state?"

Though I don't like the label, L.J. told me that this was a necessary cost of accessing services, so I reply submissively, "Yes, Dr. Horowitz."

"And you'd like a referral to an endocrinologist so you can begin testosterone therapy?"

"That's right, Dr. Horowitz."

"Fine. Please see Martin at reception and fill out the forms to have your medical files transferred to this office. Should I have any concerns upon review of your file, I will be in touch."

"Thank you, Dr. Horowitz."

"Please call me Dr. H."

Before I leave Dr. H.'s office, I make a time to move into my new apartment, then visit the restroom. Finding a bathroom in a public place is one of the challenges of being trans. To pee, or not to pee, that is the question. Whether 'tis nobler in the mind to suffer the pain of a full bladder, or venture into the men's washroom, and have some macho thug threaten to beat the crap out of you.

I check myself in the mirror. Artfully messed-up short black hair. Jeans that hang low on my hips, held in place by a belt borrowed from my brother before he wrote me off as a freak. A black cotton shirt – one size too big – that covers the lines of the wrappings that flatten my chest. A worn pair of black-and-purple Nike runners with a hole in one toe that tape will fix.

Kimmie is glad to see me move out. He helps me pack my few meager possessions, gives me a slap on the shoulders and sends me on my way.

I think I'm going to be sick. The apartment is not remotely close to the way Martin described it. The walls are a grey shade of green. The floor is hardwood that was long ago painted and is now chipping. My "den" is actually a recess in the wall. And my bamboo privacy wall has holes the size of a watermelon.

I decide to make the best of it. Where else am I going to get a place to live so close to work for two hundred dollars a month.

At work, Martin is the professional, a respected public servant. And I am the patient.

At home, things switch up. He is Martine, the diva and I am his patient servant.

"How do I look?" he asks, stuffing his already burgeoning bra with yet another sock.

"Absolutely fabulous, Martine."

Dressed as an everyday male, he is nothing special. Six foot two with skin the colour of dark chocolate, his face is nice but unremarkable. High cheekbones. Full lips. Big brown eyes that always look a bit sleepy. But when he gets out his ruby red size 14 pumps, puts on women's underwear and does his face and hair to look like Tina Turner, he is hot. Top it off with a strapless teal green silk dress with boobs to rival Dolly Parton, and I must say, he plays the part of a woman better than most women I know.

"You'll find towels and sheets in the closet next to the bathroom. Help yourself to whatever is in the fridge. Oh, and the remote for the television is on the couch, which is now your bed. Kick off your shoes and relax. I'll see you later."

I kick off my shoes. Try to relax. After five minutes, I have explored the whole apartment, flipped through all the television channels (basic cable), gone through all the cupboards and met my first cockroach. I open a can of tuna and pour a glass of orange juice. Home, sweet home.

SISTER MARY

It's Saturday and I stop into Kimmie's to see how the kid is doing. The shop is full and Kimmie is flying about, cigarillo in hand, directing traffic.

"Have a seat, please, I'll be with you in a moment. No, we do not take walk-ins on Saturday. Janice, I promise you that your husband will just die when he sees your new colour. Delores, the phone is ringing, stop flirting with the customers."

He sees me, waves hello, then gestures to the far end of the salon, scowling, I know, at the bird's nest that is my hair. Jazz is in the back, industriously applying himself to the task of doing laundry. He won't meet my eyes, offers no cordial greeting, and his face is a blank slate. I pick up a towel, and start to fold.

"I hear you've moved into your own place."

"Not exactly."

"Not exactly what?"

"Not exactly my own place."

There are strict protocols in place regarding a social workers contact with a client outside of work. Essentially, there isn't supposed to be any. But he looks so woebegone. And technically, he isn't my client any more. Once all the towels are folded and re-shelved, I make him an offer he can't refuse.

"Want to join me for lunch?" That perks him up. "How about Korean Barbeque?" He looks slightly nauseous. "Or Chinese?"

JAZZ

One week into July, and my daring leap into destiny is so far proving fruitless. I'm poor. I'm not eating well. I'm constantly tired from sleeping on the lumpiest couch in the world. And L.J. said it could take up to three months to get an appointment with the endocrinologist. So until then, I continue to be a guy in a girl's body and I hate it. No matter how hard I try to pass, how I dress, how tightly I bind my chest, how low I pitch my voice, how many repetitions of bicep curls I do, people still call me miss, gal, she.

Drastic times call for drastic measures. I decide to improvise and cut down on what I eat. Having next to no body fat will mean my face is more angular, my hips thinner and my breasts smaller. Doubling my weightlifting routine will surely bulk me up, and then if I run every day, maybe I'll stop having a period.

Kendall has been watching me. Yesterday he asked me if I have an eating disorder.

"No, I just can't afford to eat a lot."

Which is true. But not for the reasons he thinks.

L.J. didn't come to group the last night. Apparently he's busy rehearsing for his new album. There's a new guy in the support group, Heinrick from Hamburg, believe it or not, who identifies himself as intersex, whatever that means. I see Kendall once a week privately, but frankly I feel we are getting nowhere. He recommends books, gives me armfuls of educational pamphlets *so I'll be armed with knowledge.* His owl eyes follow me with concern. It curdles my stomach.

The truly sad thing is this. Sister Mary is my only real friend. And what does that say about me?

She took me out for breakfast this morning. Despite her encouragement to have a big meal, I ask for coffee, orange juice and an order of whole-wheat toast, hold the butter. The food arrives and I start to drool over the sight and smell of her Eggs Benedict. She tucks in with gusto.

"Can you pass the salt?" Chew. Chew. "Any plans for university?"

"I was accepted at U. of T. But...no money. Can you pass me the peanut butter?"

"Have you spoken to your parents about funding your education?"

"We already talked about that."

The server comes to top up our coffee. I drink mine down quickly and ask for another full cup. Better fill up on something.

"But have you asked them?"

"I told you. They cast me out."

"So dramatic sounding, like some Victorian novel. You've got a mind in there, Jazz. I just don't want to see it to go to waste."

I drop my toast down on the plate. "I've lost my appetite."

"Sorry for ruining your breakfast with pertinent questions."

"Shut up, old woman." That always makes her laugh.

As she is wiping Béchamel sauce from her face, she gets serious again. Asks what I want for myself.

"Besides a penis and testicles?" I joke, but she doesn't laugh. Instead persists, with that look in her eyes that says, don't run away from this, it is more than what hangs between your legs that will define you and you know it. Her need to make me articulate what I want brings it sharply into focus. I will never be a male like other males. I am different. I know too much about life on the other side of the gender divide. What I want for myself I can never have.

The only bright light in my life is my library card. Books. Magazines. Periodicals. My drugs of choice.

TRANSFIX: *to pierce through*

In the book *The Life of Pi*, the protagonist loses his family in an accident at sea. In the middle of the ocean, on a lifeboat that he shares with a tiger, he must use his wits to survive. I can't help but draw certain parallels between my life and this story. If I am the boy, adrift in the sea of a purposeless life, the lifeboat is Martin's apartment, the tiger is Martine. When I try to talk to him about the filthy state of the apartment, he growls. When I broach the fact that the apartment is not at all as he described it, and perhaps he could lower the rent, he bares his teeth. When I ask him if he could stop eating all my food, smoke his drugs elsewhere, and have sex at his boyfriend's apartment, he pounces. He must be bipolar or something. The flaming queen version of Dr. Jekyll and Mr. Hyde.

I've watched five different guys prance in and out of his bedroom in the last two weeks. I spy them through the holes in my Chinese privacy wall, and though I don't know any of their names, I can identify them by the sounds they make when they have an orgasm. Let's see. There's Macho Mack, who bellows like a bull moose, then drinks a beer and does it all again. Galloping Gary, who comes fast and hard like a choo-choo train, then drops into snoring slumber. Bumbling Bob ejaculates prematurely and then starts to cry. He only lasted one night. Martine's special paramour is Sultry Serje. He does his business silently. Until the big moment, when he screams so loud that once the police came to make sure that no one was being murdered.

I am adrift on a raft that is breaking apart. I have to get out of here. I need money.

I call my Auntie Nazneen. She tries to sound cool. Like she is not peeing her pants that I have finally contacted her. She invites me over for lunch.

"I'll make your favourites. Pakoras. Naan. Lamb Saag. Butter chicken. Jasmine rice." I decide to put aside my quest for the ultimate in skinny bodies and enjoy the meal.

I make myself as presentable as I can, considering I only have one pair of jeans, and two shirts – one of which is dirty. Take the subway west to Bathurst. Walk south.

Auntie floats to the door, dressed in a tangerine silk blouse, and gypsy skirt. Gold hoop earrings. A small diamond nose ring. *La Signora*, in the guise of a woman who is content.

Her living room. Just as I remember it. Spacious. Elegant. A showcase for DeBeers, all thanks to her Chief Executive Officer husband who dropped dead ten years ago, leaving her a fortune.

I visit the bathroom. Top of the line low flush toilet, a bidet and a Jacuzzi tub with gold fixtures. A large chunk of amethyst in the corner is reflected in a wall of mosaic and mirrors.

I do not look in the mirrors. I do not want to see what I have become. A beggar in my own family.

Down the stairs on plush white carpet with thick underlay. Out the back door and into the clematis-covered gazebo where lunch will be served. Tubular bells tinkle in the breeze. We sit. She pours me tea. I unroll the cutlery from the linen napkin. Comment on the beauty of the presentation, then pick up a piece of naan bread, hot from the oven.

As we eat, we tactfully avoid discussing the elephant in the middle of the room. Which leaves us very little to talk about. Over dessert, a strawberry flan, she asks about my job and where I live. I provide minimal details that do not include any specifics regarding location. She doesn't press.

When it is time to go, I do what I came here to do and ask to borrow some money. She looks concerned, then her eyes fill with tears and before I know it I'm no longer talking to *La Signora*, but to my favourite auntie who used to spoil me. When she grimaces when I tell her about the cockroaches that run over my body at night, I know she loves me as much as ever, and oh, it's been so long since I felt any love from anyone, that I almost start to cry. Almost. She takes my hand, offers me her spare bedroom.

"Come on, Auntie. You know that wouldn't work."

"I don't know why not."

But she does. She gets her purse. Pulls one, then two one hundred dollar bills from her wallet.

"I went to the bank this morning. I thought you might need a little help." Words of gratitude bubble to my lips.

But wait.

Quickly. Coyly. *La Signora* pulls her hand back. The bracelets on her arm tinkle, then settle, glittering in the afternoon sun. She uses the bills to fan her face.

"I am happy to give this to you. But you must do something in return." She tops up my teacup. Tinkle. Puts down the teapot. Tinkle. Playfully reaches out to tap my nose with her sienna painted fingernails. Double tinkle.

"Call your mother. She is worried sick. She loves you. Misses you terribly."

I should have known. Nazneen the manipulator. I fold my napkin. Replace it on the table. Stand.

"Thank you for the lunch, Signora. It was delicious, as usual."

Her brow wrinkles. "Why are you calling me Signora?" The money is still in her hand. "Jaswinder, don't be like that."

She thinks this is a game. That she has the upper hand.

Quickly. Quickly. Before I lose my nerve. Through the living room and out the front door. Take two steps in one jump onto the flagstones interplanted with thyme to make a lovely smell when you crush them under heel. Ignore Auntie on the porch. First accusing. Then demanding. Then pleading.

"Jaswinder. Please! Come back!"

A cold calm settles into me as I walk away from my once-favourite aunt, her voice growing shrill as she calls the name I will no longer answer to. She will tell my mother and father that I came begging, but that is the price I will pay for acting like a fool.

I pull my raft up to the lifeboat and peek inside, hoping the tiger is still at work. I need a few hours alone. But no. He is lying on the couch with a cloth over his head, the air heavy with the sickly-sweet smell of marijuana.

He sits up, turning to me, not tiger-eyes, but the eyes of a little lost puppy.

"Dr. Horowitz fired me! The bastard says I'm unreliable. Can you believe it?" He bursts into whooping sobs. I do what I've seen Kendall do so many times before and get him a tissue. Sit beside him. Pat him on the arm. Wish he was dead.

I have to get off the raft. And since I have no choice but to stay in this dump of an apartment, I figure…ah, if you can't beat 'em, join them. I crawl over the hull of the lifeboat and reach out my hand to take the joint the tiger is so lovingly offering. He instructs me.

"Hold your breath. Exhale slowly."

He rolls another. We repeat the entire sequence. My head starts to spin. I lie back on the couch. It is suddenly remarkably comfortable. I close my eyes and recede into nothingness. The streets are noisy, and Martine is chattering on. But inside my head is a cool and blessed quiet.

NAZNEEN

Now I see the truth about Jaswinder. She is selfish. Unkind. To run away from my home like that, without saying goodbye. She should have known that I would have given her the money. I will never forgive her.

Oh, stop it Nazneen. You will, you know you will.

Now that I think of it, perhaps I can understand. Understand that I love being a woman and if one day I looked down and saw a man's body, I would rush to the doctor and spare no expense.

All these years I just thought she wanted the privilege that goes with being a man, and nothing more. What woman doesn't?

JAZZ

Fighting to get out of a dream. Struggling with something I can't see. Trying to run away. Fly away. I wake up with a start, my heart hammering, dripping with sweat. My mouth is dry. My throat is on fire. My head hurts.

Light from the street filters through the shades, casting horizontal shadows on the pitted hardwood floor. Sounds of light traffic. A man's voice raised in anger. Springs from the couch are digging in to my back. I twist here and there trying to find comfort. In vain. I am a fairytale character in the adapted version of the Princess and the Pea.

I hear snoring from Martine's bedroom. I didn't hear him go out or come in. I must have passed out hard. His size 14 red pumps are lying on the floor in front of his door. His tiara and gloves on the windowsill.

The coffee table is next to me and I lean my weight onto it to sit up. It's pressboard. From Ikea. Covered in stains. I pad my hand over the top of it, hoping to find the bottle of water I drank from before passing out. My hand knocks over a dirty glass. Amazingly, I am able to catch it before it hits the floor. I stick my hand in the full ashtray. Grimace. Wipe the ash onto my pants. What's that? A wallet. I pick it up. Wait for my eyes to adjust to the darkness. Feel the old soft, leather ripping at the seams. I open it. Take out his credit card. Turn it over in my hand.

My gut twists. Still I do not put the wallet down. I open the fold. Count. I pull out a twenty-dollar bill. It feels alive in my hands.

A memory – of my father giving me a crisp, clean $20 bill to buy my mother a birthday present. *Something a woman would like.* He snapped the bill from his wallet. Handed it to me. Trusting.

Put the wallet down! NOW.
I have to pee. I need a Tylenol. I flick the light on in the bathroom. Roaches in formation on the wall. Ten hut! They scurry for cover. The floor is sticky, filmed over with damp. A tube of bright pink lipstick lies open on the washstand. I twist it down. Replace the cover. Pull the cord to open the blinds. A garish red. Not the red light district. Just the red light bathroom. I look out at the Brewers Retail sign across the road.
I flush the toilet and the pipes scream. The sound of snoring stops. I freeze. I hear the Wellesley bus. Smell the diesel fumes. The snoring resumes.
He won't miss $5.
I see my father's eyes – deep brown. Large. Generous. I fold the bill neatly in half. Tuck it into my pants pocket.

AMARJIT
The Hijra are the transsexual people in my country of birth, India. They live on the margins of society and must make their money any way they can – by stealing and begging, and even prostituting themselves. They face discrimination, and are often victims of violence. I don't want this life for Jaswinder!

Nazneen called today to say that Jaswinder has visited her to ask for money. Says 'he' is in trouble. That we must hire a private detective to find 'him'. I tell her no. That she has made her choice, and must live with the consequences.

I do not admit it to her. My relief at hearing some news of my daughter. And my strong conviction that if she went to Nazneen, she will soon come home.

But it can only be on my terms. I cannot call her my son. I cannot call her 'he'.

CHEMIM

For her twelfth birthday, when I gave her her first bra, she flushed it down the toilet. Our plumbing was never the same.

When she turned thirteen, she told me she liked girls. I told her that such talk was perverted. She stomped up to her room and slammed the door. Two can play at this game! I stomped upstairs and locked the door with the outside key.

That summer, she spent hours on the front porch mooning over Maddie, the sixteen-year-old girl that lived three doors down. I pulled her into the house.

"It is all over your face. The neighbours can see." She looked defiant. Proud. "Don't be foolish, Jaswinder. Maddie is dating that big football player from your brother's school. She wants a man, not a girl who pretends. You are wasting your life. No one will ever love you."

There. I said it. I could not take it back.

JAZZ

Women. So beautiful. I watch them. My favourites are the dancers from the ballet school. I love their upright backs, their long, muscled legs, their turned-out feet. Most of them have long hair, either pulled back in a ponytail or pinned up in high buns. Most of them smoke cigarettes, which I find interesting considering the rigorous physical demands of their art.

There is one that is special. She wears her long brown hair loose, and usually walks alone. Maybe she is a loner like me. From the salon windows, I watch her sitting on the bench in the parkette near the school, talking on the phone, doing her nails, smoking and drinking coffee.

After a week of staring from the shadows, of thinking about her all the time, of dreaming of her in the few hours of sleep I manage to get on the couch from hell, I decide to approach her. I borrow a cigarette from Rudolpho, Kimmie's new lover. Meander nonchalantly across the street. Think George Clooney.

"Got a light?"

She looks up. Takes me in. What does she see?

"Yeah, sure." She passes me her cigarette. I notice her long fingers. Pink nail polish slightly chipped. No rings. Big eyes. Clean face. No make-up.

"Thanks." I turn slightly away. Lighting a cigarette from another cigarette is not something I have ever done before. My hands shake slightly, but I manage to connect the end of her cigarette with mine. Inhale. Hand the cigarette back to her. *God this stuff tastes awful.* And then the burning in my lungs. *Exhale, you fool. It's not pot.*

Coughing slightly on the exhale, I muster up my courage. "You're a dancer?"

"I hope so." She lifts the cigarette. Places it between her beautiful lips and inhales like a movie star. I notice the dark circles under her eyes.

Smoothing her pink skirt over her perfect thighs, she drops her cigarette on the ground, grinds it under her heel, and then tucks a strand of hair behind her ear.

"Time for class. Have a good one." She bends, picks up her cigarette and puts it into her coffee cup. Her every movement is utterly exquisite. "Can't use the earth as my ashtray, now can I?" Environmentally conscious too. She looks me full in the eyes and smiles a wry, sad smile. My chest constricts so hard and fast, I think my heart will explode. She is walking away. Say something!

"Hey, what's your name?"

"Rosa."

ROSA

Long, brown elegant fingers. That was the first thing I noticed about him when he took my cigarette. Then worn running shoes, black jeans and a pink t-shirt that carried the logo of the hair salon I'd seen across the street. He was a small guy, with a delicate face. No beard, so he can't be more than fifteen.

We meet everyday, Monday to Friday, at the same time and at the same place. He brings the coffee. I supply the cigarettes.

I ask him questions. "Is Jazz a nickname?" He shakes his head. "Do you like jazz music?" More head shaking. "Do you have a girlfriend?" He blushes and changes the subject.

I told my boyfriend about Jazz when he came to visit on the weekend. Said that he's a nice kid.

KENDALL

Jazz has gone A.W.O.L. since our last session, which is understandable considering how I behaved. If I could go back in time and do it all again, I would.

He stomped into the room. Blurted out the question that was always foremost in his mind.

"Have you had surgery yet or not?"

If there was a question that was most frequently asked of me during the course of my long life, this would be it. Straight people. Gay people. Trans people. As if gender re-assignment surgery is the only logical conclusion. As if it would be okay in any other circumstance to ask a person about their genitals.

Maybe it was because I knew he didn't really like me. Maybe because I knew I was losing my precious objectivity. Maybe because I am so bloody tired of people asking me that question. Whatever the reason, I did not react appropriately.

"Jazz, consider this scenario if you will. You're invited to a party. You are looking forward to it. You want to enjoy yourself. Meet some new people. Talk about the book you just read, or the movie you just saw or the girl you are dating. But for reasons which you can't and will never understand, all people want to know about is what is between your legs."

"I'm confused. Why are you telling me about a party?"

He did look confused. And a little frightened of me. But I was a volcano bubbling lava.

"Yes, you are confused. And it is clear just how confused you are by the fact that you are fixated on this one issue, and somehow think that even though you have not opened up to me one iota, I should talk to you about my personal life!"

"No need to freak out, Ken. I just want to know. You always tell me to equip myself with knowledge. Are you ashamed to tell me?"

"My name is Kendall, not Ken, and…" I wasn't in the mood. I closed my daybook. Put on my jacket. Left him in my office with his jaw hanging open. I needed some lunch.

That was over two weeks ago.

Trans boys have it hard. Dominant culture still likes those labeled females at birth to stay in their place. Men on the far right on the gender spectrum do not like to see the hallowed halls of maleness, with all its implied privilege, be infiltrated by anyone without the right plumbing. I see a lot of battered faces, broken bones and worse.

He wants my help to make his outer self congruent with his inner self. Apart from the totally unprofessional need to have him like me, I want him to be safe. I have to find him. Apologize. I'm supposed to be an ally. Not a horse's ass.

TRANSGRESSION: *a going beyond, the breaking of a law, a sin*

The tiger has kicked me out of the lifeboat. And just when I thought we were getting along so well. He has accused me of stealing from him. Which is true. But it's not like he can't do without a few grams of pot, and a couple of five dollars here and there.

Whatever. I'm back sleeping on cot at the back of the salon. From the frying pan into the fire.

Sister Mary is nowhere to be found. When I call her office, Carrot-top says that she is unavailable. Yah right.

Rosa finished her course at the ballet school, and has gone home to her boyfriend in Kingston. What an idiot I am. I should have known better than to think a girl like that could want me.

Kim is not happy to have me back and is getting on my last nerve. Always making snide comments. Sticking in the knife.

"You're late. Your attitude sucks. You need to get it together."

And my favourite one. "Are you stoned?" Hell yah.

CHEMIM

She called me last night. I begged her to come home.

"Only if you accept who I am."

"That I cannot do. No."

Then she asked to borrow money.

"We cannot support you to ruin your life. No."

"Will you write a letter to the university saying that you will not pay for my tuition? So I can get a student loan?"

"After your father and I worked like dogs to save that money for you? Absolutely no!"

Then she pleaded with me to do this one thing, to tell her father that she loves him.

"Please, mother. Please."
"NO. NO. NO."

I thought that would make her come home. It did not.

JAZZ

After work today, Kim says he can no longer trust me to lock up.

"Nothing personal. But you just seem out of it." So when he leaves for the night, I am locked in.

I take a shower. Raid the fridge. Orange juice and leftover Chinese. I flip through a copy of GQ. Wish I had a good book. Wish I had money. Wish I could find a girl who would love me the way I am. Wishes. Worthless wishes. I might as well go to sleep.

A lucid dream. A nightmare. But I can't wake up.

A winter night. Starry cold. Branches heavy with snow. Roads slick with ice and salt. I am in the passenger seat of a bright yellow taxi driving along a country road. I don't know where we're going. The smell of old tobacco smoke is strong in the air though a sign on the back of the driver's seat says No Smoking.

The driver is intent on the road ahead, his fair hair greased back on his skull.

"Nice night, isn't it?" he says. Then coughs loudly. A smoker's cough. A barking sound from deep in his lungs.

A sign warns of a bridge ahead. Single lane. Only room for one car. The driver is still talking, nattering on about something. I tune him out.

"HEY! I'm talking to you." Something in his voice isn't right.

"Can you please stop? I want to get out."

A river up ahead. Frozen, except for a small serpent of open current.

"Excuse me, but I want to get out."

He speeds up. Guns the gas. The motor balks. Then responds. Lurches forward. Picks up speed.

"HEY!" Now it's me who is angry. "Let me out."

The car skids. The wheels lose traction. We slide towards the embankment. My mouth drops open. Shape of a scream. But no sound.

Time slows. The car careens off the bridge. Hits the water. Sits as if to rest before the next leg of its journey.

I want out of this dream. Please let me wake up.

Sounds of ice breaking.

Enough. I want to wake up.

More cracking sounds. The back left wheel finds water. I clamber up the plastic-covered seat. Press the button to open the window, only to discover that there is no button.

I look to the driver for help. He is gone. The back end of the car is halfway submerged. The front tires hanging onto the ice like boney fingers on a cliff face.

Please. Let. Me. Wake. Up.

Then I see it. The driver's window. Half open. I scramble forward. Knock my head on the ceiling light.

I'm going to get out of here. I shimmy through the window. First my head. Then my shoulders. My torso. No! I'm stuck. I push against the side of the car. Try to lever myself out. Icy water begins to flood in. The car is sinking fast. Is this the moment of my death?

My father taught me the Gavitri Mantra, one of the oldest and most powerful Sanskrit mantras. It is supposed to rescue the one who chants it from all adverse situations that may lead to mortality. Slowly, methodically, I repeated the sounds, phrase by phrase, employing the correct rhythm until my father's eyes glowed with pride that his daughter could so perfectly chant the ancient Sanskrit.

The mantra echoes in my mind as I struggle to wakefulness.

Om bhur bhuvha svah
Tat savitur varenyam
Bhargo devasya dhimahi
Dhiyo yo nah prachodayat

We meditate on the loving light of the God Savitri.
May his brilliance, like that of the sun, stimulate our thoughts.

It's five o'clock. An hour or so until dawn. Fresh air. I need fresh air. I pull on my jeans and start to wrap the bindings around my chest. What for? I throw the bindings to the floor, lace up my sneakers, and grab one of Rudolpho's big boots to keep the door jammed open. The air feels cool as it hits my skin, evaporating the sweat and the sick feeling left over from the dream. I walk, then jog up to the street corner, the images of the dream slowly fading. Breathe. '24/7' blares in neon from the window of Jan's convenience store. Coffee would be good. I have a dollar in my bag upstairs. I jog back.

The boot is gone. The door is locked. *Did Kimmie come in early?* I jog around the front. No lights on. Which means Kimmie isn't there and probably won't be for at least another half an hour. Which means I am locked out.

Make the best of it. I'll go for a walk. An early morning walk along Carlton before the streetcars start their daily trek across the city.

"Nice night, isn't it," a thick, slurring voice comes from a darkened doorway. I turn to see a tall, thin, dirty man. His hair is a dull yellow and is pasted back onto his skull. He is wearing a bright yellow rain slick.

"Want a smoke?" At the sound of his voice, my throat tightens and my stomach clenches. "No thanks."

Before I can move, dirty fingers grab my arm. Broken nails press into my flesh.

"HEY! What the hell do you think you are doing? Let go of me!"

He doesn't. Just coughs. A deep barking sound. Doesn't cover his mouth. A rain of spittle hits my face.

His grip is like a vise. He's younger than I thought. At least a head taller than me, and probably about forty pounds heavier. *Where are the police when you need them?*

I kick him in the shins. It feels remarkably good. I do it again. Hard. That makes him let go. I sprint across the street. Trip on the streetcar tracks. Don't fall! I jump the curb. Look behind. He's following me. Looking mad.

I pick up my pace. If I can get past the park to Sherbourne, I'll find a cop, or a taxi, or a hooker or someone who will help me.

In the park. A woman with a big dog. Just what I need. I run headlong towards her.

"Hey, I need some help here."

The dog lurches towards me, but she yanks the chain, pulling him back, and walks quickly away. For the first time in my life I wish I looked like a girl. *What was I thinking?* Women don't stop for guys in the middle of the night.

Get out of the park. Stay under the streetlights. Run. I swivel my head and out of my peripheral vision, I can see. He is still following me. My belly is cramping. I can't run much farther. *I meditate on the loving light of the God Savitri. May his brilliance like that of the sun, stimulate my thoughts. And get me the hell out of here.*

The sky is turning dawn pink. A quick glance backwards. No sign of the man in the yellow rain slick. I stop. To catch my breath. Just for a minute.

A mistake.

He grabs me. Swings me around. Slams me against a wall. He grabs my jaw. Pulls me close. His breath is hot and sour in my face.

"You hurt me."

I can't believe this. This dude thinks he is justifiably aggrieved.

I spit in his face. He slaps me hard. Once. Twice. I taste blood.

"You're a pretty little thing. Boy. Girl. Whatever you are. I got an idea. Let's take off your pants and find out."

Watching a scary part of a movie when I was a kid, my mother would tell me to relax, that it wasn't real, it was just a story. Just a story. Her voice is cool. Soft. Her hand brushes the hair from my face. *Just relax and watch the story.*

He pins me to the wall with one hand, while with the other he rips open the front of my pants. *SSSH. Watch the story.* He shoves his hand between my legs. *Relax. Watch the story.* Hear him laugh. *Relax. Just relax.* Feel him grab my hand. Pull it between his legs. *Watch the story. Watch the story. Watch the story.*

He groans. *Whispers in a shaky voice.* "Touch me."

My mother didn't know it, but she was very beautiful when she was young. I remember. Not a classical beauty. Her nose was too big and her body too sweetly plump for that. But she moved with grace, and carried a warm light within her that lit up my heart. My father was fiercely protective. Of us. Of her.

One day a man who was a colleague of my father's, an educated white man who visited our house frequently, one day this man touched my mother's hair, marveling at its beauty, then let his hand slide down the thick braid, his fingers tracing a line along her spine.

I saw my father change. From a middle-class East Indian man. Saw him grow. Become something else. A hatchet. He aimed himself at the man.

Like my father, I will be the hatchet.

He groans again. His right hand slides up the front of my shirt. Squeezes my breast hard. I fight to relax. Just enough to make him think I'm not going to fight. He jerks my pants down over my hips. *Relax.* Opens his fly. *Relax. Relax.*

Target in sight, I aim myself at him with all my might. Knee to the balls. Once. Twice. Three times.

He bellows. Doubles over. His agony feeds me.

I pull my pants up over my hips. Lock two hands into one fist. Raise them up. Bring them down. Knock his skull into the ground.

Now run. One step. Two. He grabs my ankle. I crash to the sidewalk. My head bounces. I'm okay. I kick backwards. Hit hard with my heel. Hear the sound of bone breaking. His nose. May it penetrate his rotten brain.

He lets go. Just enough. Scraping my knees along the pavement, I crawl. Push up. Hold my pants together. And run. Run. Run. *Watch the story. Watch the story. Watch the story.*

One block. Keep running. The streetcars roll, their bells clanging, rocket roosters waking up the city.

Two blocks. Ignore the cramp. Keep running. A siren. Coming for me? No.

Run. You're almost at the corner. I stop. Look back. He's gone.

I meditate on the loving light of the God Savitri. May his brilliance like that of the sun, stimulate my thoughts. I am safe.

My foot hurts. I look down. One shoe is gone. Laughing feels good.

The sun is hot on my skin, and the early morning air is muggy. My mouth is dry. A teenage girl with braces and bad skin walks by talking on her cell. She sees me. I see her see me. Bleeding. Holding my pants up with one hand. Laughing. She crosses the street. Keep moving.

I see Kimmie's face. Imagine walking into his shop, blood running from my nose, one shoe on, one shoe off. *Isn't there a nursery rhyme like that?* There should be.

The little boy walked down the lane,
One shoe on,
One shoe off,
He looked in the window and what did he see,
The face of a maniac swimming in the sea.
One shoe on,
One shoe off.
I laugh louder. Crowing. A manic Mother Goose.

Check behind you. Keep moving. My mother's voice. *Just relax.*

Sit. I'll sit. Just for a minute. Deep breath in. Deep breath out.

A hand on my shoulder. Adrenaline surge. Hatchet head up. Prepare to fight.

No need. It's a cop. One of Toronto's finest. Better late than never. His voice is muffled, like it's coming through a tunnel. Focus on his eyes. Kind eyes.

"Are you okay?"

What a stupid question. "Do I look okay?"

His partner comes up behind him.

"What have we got here?" He's big. Corpulent in fact. Too many chocolate-covered donuts. "Should I call an ambulance."

"Can you get up?" This from the kind one. The good cop.

A car honks. Another cop car. Pulling up on the curb. Asking if everything is okay. The corpulent one cracks a joke. They laugh. More jokes. How is this funny?

Focus. The good cop is talking. "We're going to take care of you here."

The corpulent one calls it in. "Female. Late teens by the look of her. Conscious but beat up. No I.D. Possible rape. Possibly stoned." The operator on the other end says something. More laughter.

NO. I lurch up. Too fast. I'm blacking out. He catches me. I gag. Stomach acid like lava up my throat. I swallow it down. "I have to get to work. I'll be fine." The last words come out slurred.

The paramedics arrive. More joking. *Is everything funny to these people?* One approaches me. A coloured girl. Mid-twenties. Pretty face. Slight accent. Sturdy. Capable. She's in charge. Tells me her name. Stella. Stella for star. Asks my name. First and last. Checks my eyes. My pulse. The cut on my head. My bleeding feet. Reports her findings to her colleague.

She asks, "Can you stand?" I try. I can't.

On to a stretcher. In to the ambulance. "I need some water." She cracks open a bottle. Smiles. Starts to joke. With me. Not at me. I drink the water too fast. Throw up on her shoe. She wipes it up. No muss. No fuss. Shit. I'm crying. She hands me a tissue. Keeps talking.

She tells me she thinks I'm cool. My haircut. The blue, pink and white streaks. I tell her I think she's cool. Her nose piercing. That she saves lives.

I've never been rolled into an emergency room on a stretcher, but I know how the scene will unfold. Like on the television show *E.R.* The rush of doctors and nurses. Surrounding me. Yelling out instructions as they ascertain the extent of my injuries. *Get her into a cubicle. Hook up the I.V.* Get down to the serious work of fixing me up. Not.

The emerg is noisy. And busy. I am one of a hundred people waiting to be seen. Stella gets me set up near a wall. I have to pee. She asks me to hold it. Leaves me by myself. Talks to the triage nurse, a sour-looking old puss. She waddles over.

"You don't have any I.D.?" I shake my head. She gives me a dirty look. Walks back to her desk, the picture of long-suffering. Stella winks at me.

"Is there anyone I can call for you?" So thoughtful. I shake my head. "Okay, just sit tight. They'll be with you shortly." She squeezes my hand. Walks away.

I want to scream, *"Where are you going? Don't go! What are they going to do to me?"* But instead I shout out, "I have to pee."

"Just hold it until they have a look at you." Then she's gone. My friend. My ally.

I sit tight. Hold my bladder. Watch the waiting room fill up. Look at the clock. It's noon. Kimmie will be freaking out. I need to find a phone.

The triage nurse comes back. Asks me to fill out some forms. I tell her I need to make a call. That I need to use the washroom. Another sour look. Cottage cheese face. Vinegar voice.

"They may want a urine sample."

"Not a problem. Give me a bottle."

"Normally we wait until the doctor has seen you."

"I'll pee on the gurney then. How's that?" Rotten cottage cheese. "Down the hall and to the left. And the pay phone is down the same hall."

"I don't have any money." More long suffering. "Come back to my desk when you're done. I'll let you use my phone if you keep it short."

Kimmie sounds irritated. "I told you I needed you to help me clean up the back room. The contractor is coming tomorrow. Where are you anyway?"

"I'm at a friend's place."

"A friend's place. Right. I didn't know you had any friends." Ouch. "Tell me the truth. Are you high?"

"Yah. As a kite." I slam the phone down so hard that Cottage Cheese jumps in her chair. Small pleasures.

Halfway through the afternoon, Jean-Paul comes in with a nasty sore throat. Dons the obligatory post-SARS mask. Takes a number. Who would have ever thought I'd be so happy to see a homeless person? I wave him over. He sits beside me on the gurney. Concerned. I tell him the annotated version of events. Describe the guy. Tell him how I kicked his nose in.

"I know that guy. A total psycho. You're lucky he didn't have a knife."

I'm lucky all right.

Paper hospital gowns. Not environmentally friendly.

"Everything off. Including your underwear." In your dreams.

A nurse comes in. Cheery. Her name is Cheryl.

Cheery Cheryl takes my pulse. Normal. My blood pressure. Normal again. Examines my head wound.

"We'll just clean this up. The doctor will check it, but I think it will be fine." Examines my foot. Swabs it clean. Gently lifts the gown. Checks the bruise on my breast.

"Oh honey, I'm so sorry," she says softly. Like we're at a funeral. Drops the gown. Gives me a cup to pee in.

"When you can, we'll need a sample."

"Sure."

"The lab technician will be in shortly. To take some blood."

"How much longer until I see the doctor?"

"We're quite backed up. It's a full moon, you know. More babies. More crazies."

"Which category do I fall into?"

I stare at a crack in the ceiling while a male doctor – a resident in need of some good acne cream – examines me. My foot. *Surface wounds.* My head. *No concussion. No need for stitches.* The bruising on my breast. *It'll be uncomfortable for a while. Use ice.*

I jump off the table. "Great. Can I go now?"

"I need to finish up the examination. I'll go get Cheryl and be back in a minute. Please take off your underwear."

He's almost out of the room and on the way to his next patient. I don't want any confusion, so I shout it out.

"No."

His face pinches. He might be the son of Cottage Cheese. "It says here on your intake form that the police suspect you were possibly raped."

"I wasn't."

"To be on the safe side, why don't I just get the rape kit."

"You can get whatever you like, but the answer is no."

"Just wait here." He disappears out of the curtain and whispers something to a woman in white orthopedic runners.

Sister Mary's voice. Loud. "Where is he?"

I am flooded with gratitude. She sweeps open the curtain. Looks me over. Doesn't mince words. "Were you raped?"

"No." She looks larger than life. Her eyes red-rimmed. Phyllis Diller hair.

"Would you tell me if you were?"

"Probably not."

"How did you know I was here?"

"You can thank Jean-Paul. What happened?"

"Get me out of here and I'll tell you."

SISTER MARY FRANCIS

A young French girl hears the voices of the Blessed Saints. They tell her that her destiny is to free her country from those who oppress her. To do this she must ride into battle dressed in men's clothes. This is against the laws of God, or so says the Church. But her voices tell her otherwise. Against all odds, she convinces the lily-livered prince – the Dauphin – to let her lead an army against the English by assuring him that God will give them victory. Which He does. But then she is captured. Tried for heresy. Found guilty. And sent to the stake. Why? Because she dared.

Jazz is such a being. He has dared. And is suffering the fiery consequences.

I slide across the plastic covered back seat of the taxi. He slides in beside me and closes his eyes.

We stop in front my humble home and I pay the taxi driver. Jazz gets out, pulling together the front of his jeans. The cut on his head is bandaged, the skin around it red and angry looking. He's got a good shiner on his right eye, and the left side of his lip is puffy. He's still wearing hospital slippers and is limping a little.

I try to take his arm, but he shakes me off. "Thanks, but I can take it from here."

It's an effort, I can tell you that. The forced bravado. I dig around in my purse. Pull out the house keys.

"Come inside."

"I have to get back to work."

"I don't think that is such a good idea. Besides, I want to show you my pad."

He's too tired to put up a fight.

JAZZ

Inside the house, away from the glare of the sun and the concerned face of the taxi driver, I am so relieved I almost start to weep. Almost. She draws the blinds. "Sit down. I'll get you some water."

Cold. Clean. I drink it down. Too fast, it hits my stomach and boomerangs straight up. First the ambulance. Now here. I haven't thrown up in such a short space of time since I had the stomach flu in grade six.

"I'm sorry."

"No need."

She goes back into the kitchen. Comes back with a cloth. Kneels to clean the floor.

"Hey, where have you been the last couple of weeks?" I try not to sound whiny.

"Writing funding applications. Meeting bureaucrats. Trying to keep the centre alive."

"Oh."

"Do you want to tell me what happened?"

"I want a shower."

She takes me up the stairs. Hands me a pile of towels and a clean robe. Doesn't talk. For which I am grateful.

Into the bathroom. Lock the door and strip.

Turn on the taps. Hot water. Lots of soap.

Wash it away. Wash it away. Wash it away.

Then sleep.

I sleep the next day through. Sister Mary brings me toast and tea and makes me eat a boiled egg. Checks the wound on my head, and gives me ice for my eye. But mostly, she leaves me alone.

The next day she insists I come downstairs. To sit out in her backyard. Get some sun. I comply, but only because I am too tired to protest. She asks me again if I want to talk about what happened. I don't.

The next morning she wakes me early. Too early.

"Wakey, wakey, sunshine. Time to rise and shine. Someone wants to meet you."

Oh no. She's found my mother. Called her. Told her everything. She's out in the hall. Waiting to descend upon me with kindness and kisses and an unspoken *I told you so*. I pull the covers over my face.

I hear the door open. Her gravelly voice saying, "Come on. Come on in, girl."

Tap-tap-tap-tap. Claws against the linoleum. Panting sounds. Sister Mary pulls the covers down. Laughs as the Labrador licks my face.

"I'm not a dog person. Make it stop!" Dog slobber on my face. Ach.

"Come here, Emma. Come on, girl." Tap-tap-tap-tap. "That's a good doggie. Now sit."

I wipe my face with a corner of the cotton sheet. "I didn't know you had a dog."

"I don't. She belongs to my neighbours, but she is a frequent visitor. I thought she might cheer you up."

"I don't want cheering up."

I push myself up to a sitting position. Look around. At the tiny room. One bed. One chair. A small table. And a wilted spider plant.

"They're hard to kill."

"What?"

"The spider plant. I see you looking at it. They're hard to kill. Want some coffee?"

"That would be great."

"Good. Get up. We're going out. If you think I'm going to let you lie here all day, re-playing whatever happened to you in your mind, you have another thing coming."

She goes into the hall, and returns with clean clothes and a pair of new sneakers. My size.

Downstairs she greets me with a glass of orange juice, and then hustles me out the door. As she is locking up, she says, "By the way, Kendall says hi. Don't look so stupid. I called him. He's meeting us for coffee. Move it, soldier."

KENDALL

I try to get a seat by the window so he doesn't feel boxed in. I try to think of what to say. What not to say. Stop thinking. Just be here. Isn't that what you tell everyone else?

The waitress arrives with new place settings.

"Coffee?"

I'd better not. I'm jittery enough. "No. Just water."

In the summer of my twenty-ninth year, I was close to finishing my PhD thesis. My friend and mentor, Doctor

Mumford, had as close to guaranteed me a teaching position at the university once I secured my doctorate. I lived in a nice little apartment just a few blocks from school, had a season's subscription for the Toronto Symphony, and was making good money by doing research for Doctor Mumford, and tutoring undergraduate students. I felt I had the world by the tail. Granted, I didn't have many friends and had never had a girlfriend since Audrey. But unlike many of alternately gendered people, I had never experienced any real violence, outside of Audrey's brother James.

One balmy summer night, Doctor Mumford gave a talk on the capacity of animals other than humans to be empathetic, to value community about individual need. He broke the mold of the common perception of nature as dog eat dog. Giving examples from his work with the Great Apes, and Rhesus Monkeys, his arguments were compelling, forcing us to look deeper into our assumed superiority about the altruistic nature of our species.

Outside of the lecture hall, I stood and watched as the groups of students drifted away, deep in conversation about the merits or lack thereof of Dr. Mumford's presentation. I felt content. A content, educated loner.

That year Doctor Mumford died suddenly of a heart attack. When he left this world, he took with him the acceptance within the academic community I had so long enjoyed as his student.

I was passed over for the teaching position I had set my sights on. And slowly, the harassment started. Just little things at first. A few practical jokes, a snide comment here and there.

Then the tempo picked up.

My office was vandalized. My car keyed. My cat, trapped and tortured and laid out on my front lawn. I had to have her put down. I reported it to the police. No one was ever charged.

I paste a bland look on my face as Jazz walks into the restaurant. I don't want him to see how shocked I am at his appearance. He sits, as far away from me as possible and will not make eye contact. Sister Mary has told me that he doesn't want to talk about what happened, and I don't want to push him.

As they place their order, I rummage around in my briefcase, pulling out the document I had bound just this morning for him. Hoping to distract him from his pain. Hoping to let him know how sorry I am for the way I acted the last time I saw him. I put it on the table in front of him.

"I brought you a copy of a personal essay I'm writing. You might find it interesting. It introduces the concept that nothing in nature is a mistake."

The waitress comes by with a coffee pot. Turns up the cups. Pours coffee. Jazz stares out the window. Sister Mary prods him in the arm. "Earth to Jazz. Come back. The good doctor has brought something for you."

He pours sugar into his coffee. Adds cream. Takes a sip. Picks up the article and reads the first paragraph aloud, making his voice labored and pompous. Is that how I sound?

A Freak of Nature? Or an Evolutionary Jump?
By K. Johnson, Ph.D.

I've been called a freak of nature. And for years I believed that to be true. A man's brain. A woman's body. How is that not an aberration?

But if every atom in my body came from a star that exploded millions if not billions of years ago, then perhaps who and what I am is simply a new way for that stardust to align, and express.

Perhaps I am not on the outside looking in, but on the outside looking out for new ways for humanity to express itself. To share with the world what I know in my heart to be true.

As it is with all living things, I am stardust. And from that place of unity, what can we not do?"

JAZZ

I am stardust. Are you freakin' kidding me? I say as much.

"Are you freakin' kidding me? Look at me, numb nuts! I was almost…raped…and surely you can imagine how particularly awful that is, you being trans and all. I'm sitting here, beat up…one side of my face looks like minced meat…I have no money, nowhere to go, and you give me a freakin' piece of paper telling me I am stardust?"

The patrons of the restaurant are looking our way. Sister Mary taps me on the arm. "Temper. Temper."

I slam my hand down hard on the table. "Please tell me, you did *not* just say…temper, temper."

She places her hand firmly over mine. Looks me straight in the eyes. "Calm down, Jazz."

Her touch burns like fire. I'm going to choke, I have to get out of here. I get up, knocking my chair back onto the floor. Spit the words out. Staccato.

"Don't touch me. Do not touch me you ridiculous excuse for an old woman. You are talking to me like I'm a baby. I expected that kind of crap from Mr. Academia over there, but not from you."

I turn to go. The waitress and I collide. She is carrying a pitcher of water, so I leave the restaurant with ice water running down the inside of my shirt. What an exit. I head down the street, first walking, then running, going who knows where. AAGH – I should have peed at the restaurant.

I throw propriety to the wind. Find a bush in somebody's front yard, squat and fertilize. The lady of the house comes out, yelling indignant obscenities with a stunning velocity that propels me up to drip dry and give her the finger before jogging away. Where to go? The world is my oyster. Down an alleyway. No, not a good idea. Out the alleyway. Out and down and right and left to wind along winding Dundas Street with the winding streetcars, and winding drunks and winding hookers. I'm winding, unwinding, re-winding. There's a sticky feeling inside of my shoe, and I know my foot is bleeding again. Who cares. I turn as I run, run as I turn, dart into traffic, not caring, not wearing my heart on my sleeve, not grieving but leaving no trace of my face in the mirror of ALL MY SORROWS. LOST TOMORROWS. BEG AND BORROW. I'm rhyming. Ranting. Screaming out loud. At strangers' faces. Empty spaces.

A small voice. A tentative tap on my shoulder. I swivel. Adopt the stance of a warrior. Trans Rambo. Ready to fight.

She covers her face with her hands. I stop when I see the little woman standing in front of me. Her arm lowers. I recognize her, her big smile with one tooth gone.

"Hewwo, Wemember me? I'm Thinthia. Fwom the thenta on Qween Stweet?" I start to laugh, a pinched, soprano sound.

She takes my hand. "Are you okay, Jath?"

The laughter rides up. Up. Up.

She pats me on the back. "Oh, no. Definitwy not. Come wif me."

The bottom of my foot is burning, probably bleeding again. I take her hand. Let her lead me. We walk south to Queen, then turn left.

"I can't walk anymore. My foot."

"We almoth there."

"I can't."

We sit on a bench. I nod off on her shoulder.

"Jath, wake up. Time to go."

The blood in my shoe has congealed. I must have been asleep for a while. I stand to find I'm light-headed.

"How much farther?"

"Not far."

We walk past the centre where I first met Sister Mary, to a large building attached to an old church, and we stop in front of a red door. I pull back.

"They can help you here, Jath. Ith a thelter. Ith thafe. I pwomise."

I'm sobbing. Big snotty sobs. Safe. I'm safe.

Summer will be over soon. In addition to my sweeping duties at the salon, I am now washing hair – for which I earn tips. Kimmie is strangely conciliatory with me in a way that tells me he feels sorry for me. I wish he didn't.

Sister Mary keeps calling. Wants to know if I'm okay. Tells me Kendall is sorry for the way he acted. That he wants to help. I tell her to leave me alone.

I eat. I sleep. I sweep. I wash and dry, then sleep. Oh Jesus, I'm rhyming again.

One day, I call home. Just for the heck of it. My brother picks up.

"Hey Sugith, it's me. Don't hang up."

Silence on the other end of the line.

"I just wanted to call to say hi." Nothing. Keep talking. "What's the news with you? How's school? You're going into your second year, right?"

"Uh-huh."

"Dating anyone?"

"No." Long pause. "Are you okay?"

I'm stunned at the question. "Yeah, I'm okay."

"It's just that…Auntie said you're in trouble. That you asked her for money to get a place to live."

"Okay, correct me if I'm wrong, but are you actually concerned about me?"

"Shove it. Tell me the truth."

"Why should I?"

"Because I'm your brother."

"That never seemed to matter to you before."

"It still doesn't. But it matters to our parents. And you're killing them. Is that what you want?"

"No."

"So tell me. Where are you? What's happening?"

I list the facts. "I have a job at a hair salon on Church Street. I make minimum wage by doing laundry and sweeping the floor, you know, general women's work, which should make you happy. When I went to see Auntie, I was in a bad living situation, but now it's all worked out and I sleep like a baby every night on a cot in the back room. Happy now?"

Sugith hangs up.

Lying in the tall grass of the ravine, I light my last joint. *Relax and watch the story*. Inhale. Hold. Exhale. *It's just a story*. The clouds. Innocently suspended on the thin line of blue.

Limbo. I am no longer a living thing. I am ice. So cold it burns. The frozen water stretches on forever to an invisible horizon. Metallic grey sky hangs heavy in an endless twilight. I call out to the sky, to the gods. To whatever is out there. Wait for an answer. Silence. I am forgotten. Forsaken.

SUGITH

I know there can't be that many hair salons on Church Street, and like it or not, I'm going to find the little freak.

It doesn't take me long. I see her through the window, sweeping her little heart out. She looks like hell. I pull out my phone.

"Auntie, I found her."

JAZZ

The salon is empty and I am cleaning up after a long workday. Kimmie has left suddenly after what apparently was an emergency call from Rudolpho.

"His flight was cancelled and he's stranded at the airport. Can I trust you to lock up?"

Alone at last. I lock the door. Pull out the rolling papers and the plant-based salvation I scored from a client earlier this afternoon. The doorbell rings. I ignore it. It rings again. Probably a product delivery. I unlock the door.

"Sugith. Auntie Nazneen. What are you doing here?"

La Signora and her sidekick regard me coolly from behind sunglasses, their arms crossed in front of their chests. *Men in Black* with a twist. As one, they pull the sunglasses from their faces. Step towards me. He angry. She concerned. Saying the same thing at the same time but with different intent.

"What happened to you?"

"Nothing for you to worry about."

Sugith pushes past me, into the salon. Typical. Auntie stands on ceremony. Waits in the doorway. "Aren't you at least going to ask me in?"

"Of course, Auntie. Come in."

Sugith throws himself down on the new hot pink leather couch, and stretches out in holiday cruise position.

"Nice place you got here. Who's that up on the wall?"

"Freddy Mercury. The lead singer of Queen."

"'We are the champions'?"

"Yeah, that's the one."

Auntie Nazneen clears her throat. "Jaswinder...er, Jazz. Let me get right to the reason we have come. We want you to come home with us."

I choke back the bile that rises in my throat. "No way."

"Your mother is not well."

"What's wrong? Is she sick?"

"It is her heart. She is dying of a broken heart."

I roll my eyes. I can hear my mother saying those very words. "You can tell her I'm okay."

"You can tell her yourself. Sugith and I are prepared to take you by force if necessary."

My Auntie drives a 1998 Lexus, very posh, with black leather seats, and an expensive sound system. The strains of Vivaldi's "Four Seasons" play as we turn onto the Gardiner Expressway, and before long, Sugith is sawing logs on the back seat. It is a sound I remember from my childhood. Noisy, but somehow comforting.

"What happened to your face?"

I play with the bass and treble on the stereo. "How's Dad?"

"Don't change the topic. Your father is fine. As I was saying…"

"Will he be there?"

"No."

That's a relief. And a disappointment.

"Did someone beat you up?"

"Some jerk on the street. It's no big deal. I'm fine."

Oh no, she's going to cry.

"I do not understand why you cut your mother and me from your heart."

Looking closely, I can see that my aunt does not seem to have suffered the ravages of time. Her skin is still smooth, her hair full and dark – even if it did come from a bottle. Her hands are the only things that show her age, the skin. No longer taut, the veins are larger. Many of her knuckles are swollen.

"Are you listening to me, Jaswinder?"

"I am listening, Auntie." I concentrate on the skyline. The billboards. The view of the Exhibition.

"My feelings were hurt so badly when you ran out on me."

I know what she wants. An old-fashioned heart to heart. I'm not going to give it to her. We ride in silence for the rest of the trip. I count the exits. Islington. Kipling. 427/ Brown's Line. Dixie Road. Right turn signal on. Slow down. Drive north. Past the Dixie Value Mall. Past Value Village. Left on Burnamthorpe. Then right. Then…the familiar driveway. Auntie Nazneen reaches over to put her hand on my arm.

"The truth is…when you came to see me, I wanted to help, though I went about it badly. After you left my house that day, I called your father, told him that you were in trouble. But Amarjit...he is stubborn. And when you did not come home, he forbade your mother and me to even speak of you. And like the fools that we are, we did not challenge him."

The house looks much the same. However, my mother looks older by ten years. Dark circles under her eyes. A slash of bitterness between her brows. Grey hairs where there were none.

She pats the seat on the sofa beside her. "Come here. Please. Sit beside me, Jaswin...Jazz." The name sounds funny in her mouth. "Let me look at you." Tentatively, she reaches her hand forward. Grazes the bruise on my face. Forces her lips into a smile. "She looks well except for...she looks well, does she not, Sugith?"

Before he exits stage left, Sugith whacks me on the back between my shoulder blades. Never too late for a show of brotherly love. "She looks like crap."

"He's right, mom."

She fixes her eyes on my face. "You do not look like crap. Nazneen, would you bring us some tea? I want a moment alone with...my son."

She takes both of my hands into her own. They are cold but surprisingly strong. "I owe you an apology."

"Mother. Don't."

"No, let me finish. I knew when you were little that you were different. I knew it in my heart, but I did not want to know what I knew, and in that I betrayed us both."

My mouth is dry. "Mother, I..."

"Don't interrupt me now. Nazneen will be back with the tea very soon, and I have more to say. I see in you great courage. The courage to strive to be who you really are. If I had respected that courage...well, just imagine what your life would have been."

I don't want to imagine that. I pull my hands away and find I am suddenly and fiercely angry. I swallow the rage down. There's no point in it now. It's too late.

"What happened is in the past. It's over. It doesn't matter."

"Oh, but it does. And I am sorry. Can you forgive me? Can you forgive your old mother for what she could not do?"

TRANSPARENCY: *A state of being transparent, that which can be seen through, easily understood, a picture seen by allowing the light to shine through.*

You are woman; you are man; you are boy and you are girl;
you are the shivering old man helped by a stick;
you are born in the form of this world.
You are the blue butterfly, the green-eyed parrot and the
lightning cloud.
You are the seasons and the seas.
You are the one without any beginning; you are omnipresent;
all the worlds are born out of you.
– Shvetashvatara Upanishad

KENDALL

Jazz is standing at my office door. Without an appointment. His hair is longer, and he is painfully thin. But he looks somehow stronger.

I gesture for him to sit down. He stays standing.

"I finally got an appointment with the endocrinologist. I want to talk to you about what questions to ask."

I know he could find this information on his own. But he's come to me.

He sits down. Regards me with wary eyes. Waiting. I tell him I'm glad to see him. He nods. We talk about his appointment, and I write out a list of questions, clarifying as I go.

After half an hour I look up. "Anything else you want to know?

"No, I'm good."

"You know that testosterone has lots of potential side-effects that you won't like."

"You mean I might end up sweating like a pig, like you?"

"That is possible."

"And gaining extra weight."

"Maybe."

"And speaking in long convoluted sentences?"

I had that coming. "Well, no."

"And telling people that they are stardust?"

I grin like a Cheshire cat. "Highly unlikely. But, I wouldn't rule it out."

JAZZ

A list of people who are in my corner, and will support me no matter what I choose.

> My mother
> Auntie Nazneen
> Sister Mary
> Kendall
> L.J.
> Kimmie
> Cynthia

> On the bench but coming around.
> Sugith

Still stubbornly entrenched in his position, but I am hopeful.

> Father

Jean-Paul has disappeared, but I know where he would stand. I hope he is safe.

I'm moving into some transitional housing until I can find something more permanent. Kimmie is teaching me how to cut hair, so I can earn extra money. I'll need it. T. is expensive. And no more reefer madness. I want to be present as my body changes.

Below me, the ice shifts, cracks. Sounds of water flowing. The glowering sky recedes to reveal a startling blue and the crisp chill turns tail and, like a guilty child, runs away. Before me, a small bridge waits. From a distance, I hear the sound of singing. On the horizon I see a band of people. Some known. Some unknown. Calling to me with open arms. Inviting me into the future that awaits me.

Kendall says...*If every atom in your body came from a star that exploded billions of years ago, then perhaps who and what you are is simply a new way for that stardust to align. An evolutionary leap exploding normal into the countless, diverse ways that life seeks to express itself.*

I am life seeking to express itself. I like that.

There is a shadow of a girl floating around me. Gossamer. Guileless. And though I cannot unlearn or forget what her life in me has taken, what it has given is an inestimable gift.

There is a shadow of a boy walking within me. His spirit is lightning fire. He will not be shackled. I give him the lead. His heart thrums in anticipation of his victory.

At birth, I was labeled a girl.

At the hour of my death. I will be buried as a man. But I am so much more.

My name is Jazz. Like the music, I am nature's improvisation.

RESOURCES

The 519 Community Centre provides programs and advocacy for people in the LGBTT2SQI communities.
http://www.the519.org/

EGALE Canada Human Rights Trust promotes LGBT human rights through research, education and community engagement.
http://egale.ca/

The Safe Zone Project helps people who want to educate others on LGBTQ, gender, and sexuality issues.
http://thesafezoneproject.com/

The Genderbread Person is a *tasty little guide* to help us understand gender.
http://itspronouncedmetrosexual.com/2012/03/the-genderbread-person-v2-0/

Transgender 101 – A simple guide to a complex issue. A great resource book written by a social worker, popular educator, and member of the transgender community, Nicholas M. Teich / Columbia University Press.

ACKNOWLEDGEMENTS

This is a work of fiction. Any resemblance to real characters or events is purely coincidental.

The story is set in the late 1990s in the city of Toronto. Though many of the locations mentioned are real, many are the product of my imagination and may bear little resemblance to the real thing – most particularly the 519 Community Centre, where a group of dynamic and committed individuals have worked tirelessly to create a safe and healing space for those in the LGBTQ community. More information on the Centre can be found in the resource section at the back of the book.

Over the years, I have had the pleasure of working with many wonderful people of East Indian descent. To the best of my abilities, I have attempted to provide an authentic portrayal of Jazz's family and culture. I apologize for any inaccuracies.

Many thanks to the folks at Quattro Books for believing in this book. Thanks to my family, friends and community. Your support has been invaluable.

Lastly, none of this would be possible without my husband, Glenn, and my daughter, Faith. The light that shines from both their hearts has kept my own little light burning strong.

Other Quattro Fiction